A BRAINSTORM

Stevie's mind began to race. "Uh, wait a second," she said. "I just got an idea."

Carole caught the look in her friend's eye. Sometimes it meant trouble, but it also meant fun. "Is this a Saddle Club meeting?" she asked.

Stevie nodded. Carole glanced at Lisa, Kate, and Christine. Wordlessly, the five girls formed a circle so they could talk in private.

"So?" Stevie asked.

"I say we do it," Carole said.

"Me, too," Lisa agreed.

Kate and Christine nodded.

Lunch was delayed for a half hour while The Saddle Club registered for the barrel-racing event in the rodeo.

"Name?" the woman behind the desk asked.

"The Bar None Riders!" Stevie answered. Smiles from her friends confirmed their approval.

"Here are your numbers and your instructions," the woman told them. She gave the package to Christine.

They were in!

THE SADDLE CLUB

RODEO RIDER

BONNIE BRYANT

BANTAM BOOKS
NEW YORK · TORONTO · LONDON · SYDNEY · AUCKLAND

Tip of my hat,
and a special thank-you to Don DeMarzio.

RL 5, 009–012

RODEO RIDER
A Bantam Skylark Book / September 1990

ISBN 0-553-15821-X

Published simultaneously in the United States and Canada

PRINTED IN THE UNITED STATES OF AMERICA
OPM   0 9 8 7 6 5 4 3 2 1

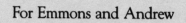

For Emmons and Andrew

"TELL ME MORE about Kate," Carole Hanson said eagerly. She was sitting at the kitchen table with her father, Colonel Hanson, and his best Marine Corps buddy, Frank Devine. Frank was now retired from the Corps and lived with his wife, Phyllis, and their daughter, Kate, on a dude ranch. Carole and her two best friends—who were horse crazy just like Carole— had once visited Kate there. They could hardly wait until they could go again. But that wasn't going to happen as long as school was going on and until they figured out how they'd pay the airfare from Washington, D.C., near where they lived in Willow Creek, Virginia.

"Kate's fine," Frank told Carole. He handed her an envelope. "I almost forgot to give you this letter she wrote you and Stevie and Lisa." Carole tucked the envelope in her pocket to read later with her two best friends. Frank continued talking about his daughter, and Carole didn't want to miss a word. "She's been working like crazy on her roping. Eli's got her all excited about rodeo stunts like that. So far, though, all she can rope is a lot of dirt. The stray heifers on our land are safe from her lariat!"

Eighteen-year-old Eli Grimes was one of the wranglers at the Devines' ranch, The Bar None. Carole had seen him rope and she could imagine how hard it was to learn to use a rope that well. But she also knew that Kate Devine, former junior champion in English riding, had all the determination necessary to learn anything when it came to horses.

Carole listened raptly as Frank told them more about The Bar None. The memories of her wonderful visit there came back to her in a flood. She felt almost homesick for it. Frank's stories were nice, but it wasn't the same as being on the ranch.

"So how are things going at the ranch, Frank?" Colonel Hanson asked.

"Sometimes dude ranching makes the twenty-mile marches in the Marine Corps seem like a Sunday picnic!" Frank joked. But Carole had the feeling that he wasn't really kidding around. She exchanged a quick glance with her father, who apparently felt the same edge to Frank's remark.

"Tough, huh?" the colonel asked sympathetically.

"Nah, it's an easy life. Getting up before dawn, taking care of livestock, managing a staff, fixing everything that breaks—and believe me, *everything* breaks—all that's easy. The tough part . . ." Frank paused, reconsidering what he was about to say. "Actually, there isn't a tough part. Phyllis and Kate and I are having a whale of a time."

Carole knew he was trying to be reassuring. Somehow, though, she didn't feel reassured. Something was wrong, but Frank wasn't going to tell them what it was.

Although Frank had retired from piloting in the Marine Corps, he now earned extra money flying a private plane for a wealthy rancher who had business interests in Washington. Carole had seen him twice since she'd last seen Kate.

"Why don't you bring Kate with you next time?" she suggested. "Would Mr. Lowell let you?"

"Sure he would, but I couldn't do it. There's a little thing you've probably heard of—school?" Frank grinned. "But that gives me an idea. Why don't you come back with me when I leave tomorrow? There's going to be a rodeo in Two Mile Creek next weekend. It's pretty exciting stuff!"

For a second, just a second, Carole thought her father might let her go. After all, the only thing she'd miss at home would be school. . . .

"Don't tease her, Frank," Colonel Hanson said. "If I let Carole do whatever she wanted, she'd spend all of her time with horses—all over the world, if she could. It may be possible for her to come out to visit next summer, but, until then, she's got something much more important to do. . . ."

"Yeah, I know: school," Carole said, completing her father's boring thought. She didn't like it, but she knew a fact when she saw one.

"Well, I'll make you a promise, Carole," Frank said. "The next time you and your friends decide to come, I'll arrange to fly you girls round trip in Mr. Lowell's plane."

"That would be fabulous!" Carole said. She could hardly believe what she'd just heard. "I guess it pays to have friends in high places—like twenty-five thousand feet high!"

"Oh, Frank, you don't have to do that," Colonel Hanson said.

"Oh, yes he does!" Carole said without thinking. Both her father and Frank gave her surprised looks, and then burst out laughing.

"It's no problem," Frank told Carole and her father. "Besides, I need the flying hours. We could probably coordinate two of Lowell's trips to Washington with one round trip of yours to Two Mile Creek."

"Wait'll Stevie and Lisa hear about this," Carole announced excitedly. She stood up. It was almost time to leave for her riding class. She gave her father a hug and then gave one to Frank Devine, too, since he would be leaving the next morning.

"What a hug!" Frank said.

"Some of it's for Kate," Carole explained.

"I'll see to it that she gets it," Frank promised.

AT FIRST, CAROLE barely noticed the cold as she waited for the bus to take her to Pine Hollow, the stable where she and Stevie Lake and Lisa Atwood rode horses. It was one of Carole's favorite places. The girls not only rode there, but they also had all the opportunities they wanted to take care of horses. As a way of keeping expenses down and making riding an activity more people could do, Pine Hollow required its riders to help with the daily chores. Carole could learn everything about horses, from grooming them, cleaning their stables, even training the stable's youngest tenant, a foal named Samson, to cleaning tack and studying horse care and stable management. Carole wasn't certain what she wanted to be when she grew up, but she knew it would definitely have something to do with horses. Her career possibilities included trainer, owner, breeder, vet, rider, even champion. Maybe all of them, Carole mused.

Then a gust of wind came and seemed to cut right through her warm jacket, sending a chill down her spine. It was winter, all right, although usually the Virginia winters were relatively mild. The gray afternoon sky seemed unusually menacing. Carole tugged her scarf up over her chin and tried to ignore the weather. She warmed herself with thoughts of The Bar None and The Saddle Club.

The Saddle Club was a group she had founded with Stevie and Lisa. It had only two rules: All the members had to be horse crazy, and they had to be willing to help one another out of trouble—horse trouble, homework trouble, even boy trouble. So far, the three founders were the main members of The Saddle Club. An official out-of-town member was Kate Devine, who lived a few thousand miles away. On their next trip to The Bar None, the girls planned to invite another girl, Christine Lonetree, to join the club. She was a Native American girl they'd met near the ranch. Christine's dog, Tomahawk, had been killed saving Stevie from a rattlesnake.

The bus arrived and Carole shook off her thoughts. This was no time to think of The Bar None. There was no way she'd be going there for at least six months. She had to concentrate on today.

"MERCURY'S DROPPING SOMETHING awful," said Red O'Malley, Pine Hollow's primary stablehand, greeting Carole at the door.

"Then we'll have to bed the horses down carefully after class," Carole said. When it came to horses, Carole was all business and she never shirked her responsibilities. She headed for the tack room to find Stevie and Lisa.

Both girls were already there, picking up the tack to

get their horses ready for class. "I've got a letter to us from Kate!" Carole announced happily, waving the envelope in the air.

"Oh, great!" Stevie exclaimed, her eyes dancing. Stevie, whose real name was Stephanie, was the most animated person Carole knew. The problem was keeping her still sometimes! Stevie had a weird sense of humor and a love of practical jokes that sometimes got her in a lot of trouble. In fact, it often got her friends in trouble right along with her. Carole and Lisa didn't usually mind, though. Being anywhere with Stevie, even in trouble, was almost always a lot of fun.

Lisa Atwood seemed to be Stevie's exact opposite. She was a little older than Stevie and Carole, but she didn't look it. She had light brown hair and always dressed neatly and fashionably, unlike Stevie, who seemed to own nothing but jeans. Lisa was the newest rider of the three, but was an apt pupil at riding, as she was at everything else, and had quickly become as horse crazy as her friends.

The three girls thought it would be impossible to find three people more different than they were. But when it came to friendship, their differences weren't nearly as important as their similarities. They all loved horses, and that was enough to bind them together.

"So, what did Kate say in her letter?" Lisa asked.

"I don't know," Carole told her. "I haven't read it yet. I wanted to save it until we could read it together." She started to open the envelope, then changed her mind and slipped it back in her pocket. "Nah," she said. "There are just a few minutes until class. We'll read it while we're doing chores."

"You mean *you'll* read while *we* pitch straw?" Stevie teased.

"Well, you're so good at pitching straw . . ." Carole began.

"Oh, flattery will get you everywhere!" Stevie said. "Tell you what. I'll show you my secret to pitching straw and then *I* can read while *you* pitch straw."

"Max will have us all pitching straw until midnight if we're late," Lisa said sensibly.

On that note, the three girls got their horses' tack and went to work. Max could be very grumpy when students were late to class.

"BALANCE MAY BE the single most important factor in successful riding," Max declared to the class.

Lisa could believe that. She just hoped she had enough balance to stay on the horse she was riding until the end of the exercise!

The class was riding at a sitting trot, with no stirrups, holding the reins with one hand. Their left hands were behind their backs.

"Reach up with those left hands as if you're trying to scratch!" Max told them.

Lisa tried to do it. Somehow, reaching with her left hand made her sit straighter. Her legs hung lower and her balance was better. She gripped firmly with her thighs. It was working!

"Nice, Lisa," Max said. "Now stay like that. Good job."

Lisa beamed to herself. Compliments from Max were rare, indeed. She felt good.

"Okay, now, down to a walk, let the horses cool down, and then class is over."

Isn't that typical? Lisa thought to herself. The minute she got the hang of something, it was time to stop. She wanted to be able to remember the feeling of doing it right so she could do it the next time she rode.

"We have extra chores this afternoon," Max announced as the ten horses in the class circled him at a cool-down walk. A few students groaned in protest. "It's cold and getting colder, so we have to blanket the horses and bed them down carefully."

"IF ONE MORE person tells me the temperature, I think I'm going to scream!" Stevie announced over the stall that separated Topside, the horse she rode, from Pepper, the one Lisa rode.

"So, what was it last time you heard?" Lisa asked.

"Twenty-one, down from twenty-eight ten minutes ago."

"That *is* cold."

"Did you hear?" Meg Durham asked excitedly, poking her head over the stall on the other side. "It's only fifteen degrees out—and it's going down to zero!"

A muffled scream came from Stevie's side of the wall.

Lisa slipped a quilted blanket over Pepper's back and began tying the strings that would hold it on.

"Horses don't mind the cold, you know," Stevie said, peering over the wall as she put Topside's blanket on. "They're outdoor animals. A lot of these guys' ancestors lived on the plains where it gets a lot colder than this."

"But these horses are in stalls and can't run around to keep warm," Carole reminded her from across the stable's hallway. "Also, it was their *ancestors* running around on the frozen plains. These horses are used to indoor temperatures. So that means, be sure to give them lots and lots of warm straw, and fasten the blankets on snugly."

"Enough, enough," Stevie complained. "We get the picture!"

She sounded very cranky, and Lisa had the feeling that Stevie was about to go into a major grump. "I've got an idea, Carole," Lisa interrupted, quickly changing the subject. "Isn't this a good time for you to read Kate's letter?"

It turned out that it was. Carole was finished with her grooming and waiting for her friends to finish so they could all do the stable chores together. She pulled the letter out of her pocket and began reading. Kate sounded well. She started by telling the girls about the upcoming rodeo. It was a one-day event, but it was the only rodeo Two Mile Creek had and it sounded like a lot of fun.

Then Kate described her roping lessons. She made

them sound totally hopeless. The girls knew better than that.

"If I know Kate, she'll be able to rope a pea at fifty yards within a month," Stevie remarked. Lisa was inclined to agree with her.

Kate concluded her letter with a strange statement: "So, as you can tell, we're all having a lot of fun here. Dude ranching agrees with Mom and Dad and me. I just hope we'll be able to continue to do it. Cross your fingers for us, okay?"

"What does that mean?" Stevie asked. Lisa shook her head, concerned.

"Something is definitely wrong," Carole said. "Frank hinted at it when he was talking with my dad, but then tried to pretend nothing was the matter."

"That's it, then. Whatever it is, it's bad," Stevie said.

"Okay, so what are we going to do about it?" Lisa asked, feeling frustrated by the circumstances.

Both girls looked at Carole for an answer.

Carole frowned. "I'd like to tell you I think this is a good Saddle Club project, but I have a sneaking suspicion that this one may be too big—even for us—especially when we don't know what it is that we're up against."

"Since when did that ever stop us before?" Stevie asked.

"Did you hear?" Red O'Malley said, interrupting their conversation. The girls looked at him. "Temperature's still dropping. We've got one major ice storm on our hands!"

All thoughts of The Bar None fled their minds. There was suddenly too much work to do at Pine Hollow.

THE NEXT MORNING when Carole woke up, she ran to the window to look out. When she'd come home the night before, the world had seemed frozen. Tree branches were coated with thick layers of ice, which almost seemed to protect them against the frigid weather that had come so suddenly.

But now, there was no winter wonderland. As fast as the freeze had come, it had gone. The ground was soggy, strewn with twigs and branches that had snapped off from the weight of the ice the night before. The sun shone brightly. All that was left of the storm was a mess.

"Rats," she said out loud. She had been hoping for something serious enough to close school. A day off could be lots of fun . . .

Then she heard her clock radio click on. There was an extended news report about the storm's damage.

". . . the whole area was totally unprepared for the sudden deep freeze. All over the county, telephone and electrical lines are down and pipes have frozen and cracked. The worst hit was Willow Creek, where construction work bared pipes leading to the municipal center, including the town hall and the junior high school, as well as other local buildings. Damage is so severe"—Carole held her breath—"that authorities are telling workers not to come in, except for emergency personnel. Schools will be shut down. The mayor was unable to say when schools would reopen, but said repairs would take at least a week. In a related incident . . ."

A week! No school for a week!

Carole whooped.

"Heard the good news on the radio, eh, sweet thing?" her father called up the stairs.

"Can you believe it? What am I going to do first?"

"Pack, I'd say."

Pack? What was her father talking about? "Where are we going?" she asked.

"Not *we*, *you*. And Lisa and Stevie," Colonel Hanson said. "I mean as long as the schools are shut—and even Stevie's fancy private school suffered bad damage with the downtown water disaster—you three are just going to have to get out of your parents' hair. I just got off the phone with the Atwoods and the Lakes. The only thing we could all think of was to send you off to the sunny Southwest, with a trained Marine Corps pilot. Frank'll bring you three back next Sunday when he comes to pick up Mr. Lowell. Now, he's staying over an extra day to wait until the congestion eases up at the airport. Think you can be ready to go by tomorrow morning—at O-eight hundred?"

For a moment Carole was speechless. Then she grinned broadly. "Does a private first class polish brass?"

No problem!

THE FLIGHT WITH Frank Devine in the small plane went very smoothly. The last time the girls had flown to the ranch, they'd had to take three different airplanes. They thought this new way was a lot easier, and a lot more fun.

"Tray tables and seat backs into their full upright and locked positions?" Stevie joked. Of course, there wasn't room for tray tables in the little plane, and the seat backs only reclined a few inches. It was Stevie's way of saying that she thought the end of the trip was near. Stevie glanced out the window and spotted the small airport a few miles away. Another advantage to flying with Frank was that they could land at a local airport, which was just ten miles from the ranch, instead of the nearest commercial airport, which was over seventy miles away.

Frank laughed. "All you really need to do is make sure your seat belts are on—oh, and extinguish all smoking materials."

The girls giggled.

"There's the airport!" Carole said excitedly.

"And there's Kate!" Lisa said, almost bouncing in her seat.

Stevie squinted out her window at the bright desert sunlight. She could just make out two small figures standing by the little terminal building who might be Kate and Eli. A pickup truck was parked on the other side of the building.

The plane slowly made its descent. Even though the airport was small, with no other visible air traffic, Frank kept in constant touch with the tower, receiving all his landing instructions and following them carefully. He concentrated totally on the task in front of him. Stevie watched his hands flick busily over the numerous switches and buttons on the panel in the cockpit. She couldn't make any sense of what he was doing. She decided to concentrate on the approach instead.

The figures were becoming clearer. "It's Eli! I know it is. And Mel is with him!" Stevie cried. Mel was Eli's favorite herding dog. She was caramel-colored and had had a litter of puppies the last time the girls had been at the ranch. Now she sat motionlessly next to Eli, who watched the approaching plane. His big cowboy hat shaded his eyes.

Kate stood on his other side. In contrast to Eli's calm, Kate was jumping all over the place and waving excitedly. Stevie wished she could be jumping, too. She had the feeling, though, that it might distract their pilot. And the last thing in the world she wanted to do was to distract their pilot!

Almost imperceptibly, the plane slowed down and settled onto the runway. When it was at taxiing speed, Frank made a U-turn. Within seconds, they had stopped in front of the little building that served as the airport terminal.

Kate ran up to the plane and helped from the outside as Frank opened the door.

The girls couldn't get out of the plane fast enough. They were eager to see Kate and to hug her. Stevie was dimly aware of Eli and Frank unloading their luggage as the four of them had their reunion on the tarmac. It was so exciting to be back with Kate, headed for The Bar None.

"Can we have the same cabin we had before?" Carole asked.

"You can have your pick of cabins, except for the one with the broken toilet and the other with the leaky roof—or is that two now with leaky roofs?" Frank said. Stevie thought there was something odd in his tone.

"It's not that bad, Daddy," Kate said. "Just one leaky

roof. Besides, we've got some guests coming for the rodeo on the weekend."

The three other girls exchanged troubled looks. Something was definitely wrong at The Bar None, and they were beginning to get an idea of what it was. It was time for action. They hadn't come a moment too soon. Stevie and her friends looked around for their bags.

"We've got to get to the ranch," Carole announced, picking up her carry-on bag.

"Right, we've got to talk," Lisa said.

Frank looked at them curiously. "Why, you've done nothing but talk for the last six hours in the plane!" he teased.

"That was just *talk*," Stevie said. "This is business."

"Saddle Club business," Lisa said. Then she turned to Kate. "Are you ready for your first official meeting since joining?"

"You bet I am!" Kate replied. She picked up one of Lisa's suitcases and loaded it on the truck. The group began the ten-mile trip to The Bar None.

THE BAR NONE looked just the same as the day The Saddle Club had left it a few months before, except for one thing. In the summer, it had been full of paying guests. Now, just two guests occupied one of the cabins. The place looked empty, almost deserted.

"The trouble is that we have all the expenses and none of the income," Kate said, answering her friends' question before it was asked.

"But isn't this just the off-season?" Stevie suggested. "I mean, it'll fill up again at vacation time, won't it?"

"Maybe," Kate said. She paused. "Did you notice all the signs along the roadside for The Dapper Dude Ranch?"

"Who could miss them?" Stevie remarked. "They seemed to be up every fifteen feet."

"They *were* up every fifteen feet," Kate said disgustedly. "It's a new place that's opened up right outside of town. They're advertising all over the place—not just on the roadway, but in magazines and with slick brochures. It seems like they have all the money in the world to bring in business. They've certainly managed to take a whole lot of business away from us. We've even had people cancel reservations here and say they'd decided to stay at The Dapper Dude instead. Can you imagine?"

"I can't imagine wanting to stay at a place called The Dapper Dude. It's the stupidest name I ever heard of," Stevie said.

"To you, maybe," Kate replied. "But the fact is, whatever they're doing, it's working, and The Bar None is in trouble. It's lucky for us that The Dapper Dude is all booked up for this weekend because of the rodeo. We're getting their overflow. For now, anyway, we're still in business. After next week, well, we just don't know."

It was a sobering thought, casting a pall on their reunion. With Kate's words echoing in each of their minds, the girls completed their unpacking. Three words kept running through Stevie's head as she worked—Saddle Club project.

But, really, what could they do?

IT WAS ABOUT four o'clock by the time they finished unpacking. Since there seemed to be little to say or to do about The Bar None's predicament, Kate suggested that they head for the barn, where they could enjoy themselves instead of sitting around and worrying over something they couldn't do anything about. The other girls agreed, a little relieved to set aside the problem for a while.

"Hey, look! Eli's practicing for the rodeo," Kate said, leading them over to the corral. "It's really neat, once you figure out what he's doing."

Stevie watched carefully. Eli mounted his horse, got him into a spurt of a gallop, made him stop so fast that the animal had to dig his hooves into the ground, leaped off him while he still seemed to be in motion, and ran forward, which somehow made the horse back up.

"What is he doing?" Lisa asked, posing the question for all of them.

They drew up to the edge of the corral, joining a girl about Eli's age who was leaning against the round wood fence.

"Girls, this is Jeannie Sanders, our new wrangler," Kate said. They all nodded and shook hands, but it was clear that Jeannie's attention was on Eli.

"How's he doing?" Kate asked.

"Oh, *wonderfully*," Jeannie answered, almost breathlessly. Then she blushed.

Stevie didn't usually think of herself as a person with a lot of insight about what was going on in other people's minds, but she certainly knew a Grade A crush when she saw one. There was no doubt that Jeannie had one of those on Eli. The girl could barely keep her eyes off of him.

"More important, *what's* he doing?" Stevie asked.

"He's practicing his stopping and dismounting and getting his horse to work with him for calf roping. See, the cowboy not only has to rope the calf, but he's also got to get three of its legs tied together. To do that, he has to immobilize the calf. And the horse helps him by keeping the lasso rope taut. See how the horse backs up after Eli's dismounted? That's what he's supposed to do because, believe me, the calf is struggling to get away from both the cowboy and the horse. This is a very tricky event. It's the one that calls for the most coordination between the cowboy and his horse. For something like steer wrestling, muscle is what counts the most. For saddle-bronc riding, well, that's mostly experience and balance. Calf roping, now that calls for skill."

She sighed as she said the last words. Stevie took it to mean that, in Jeannie's opinion, Eli had all the skill anybody could ever ask for, at everything.

While they watched, Eli brought out a calf and let him run loose in the corral while Eli practiced his roping. The girls already knew Eli was really good at that.

It was fun to watch and they all enjoyed it, nobody more than Jeannie.

"Eli's in three events on Saturday: steer wrestling, calf roping, and bronc riding. And there's an awful lot hinging on his riding," Kate told her friends. "He's counting on his performance to get him a rodeo scholarship at the state university. We're counting on it to be good publicity for The Bar None. It could really make a difference to all of us."

"He sure looks good to me," Stevie said, admiring Eli's skill. Jeannie looked a little jealous. Stevie thought it was probably just an automatic reaction. "I mean, he looks like he could win," she corrected herself quickly.

"Let's go see if your mother needs any help with dinner," Stevie suggested. When they were beyond Jeannie's hearing, she raised the question that was really on her mind. "I know Jeannie's in love with Eli. I've never seen such a love-struck doe in my life, but does he know she's alive?"

"Nope," Kate said. "She trails after him like a puppy and he never seems to notice her at all. I mean, he likes her okay. They work together just fine, but what I think we're seeing here is pure unrequited love."

"Sad," Carole remarked. "She's so, so . . ." she struggled for the right word.

"Adoring," Lisa supplied. "And all that adoration shouldn't go to waste!"

"Now there's a project worthy of The Saddle Club," Stevie said, her eyes sparkling with excitement. "First, we have to get them together, alone. Moonlight, stars—you know the routine. And then . . ."

"I wouldn't get so carried away," Carole advised. "Why not let nature take its course?"

Stevie grinned impishly. "On some things, Carole, nature can be very careless. This is going to require something more than that!"

STEVIE OPENED HER eyes. At first, she couldn't see anything. The bunkroom was completely dark. She glanced at the luminous clock on her bedside table. The clock said it was five-thirty. It was seven-thirty back in Willow Creek. Her internal clock was telling her to get up. The bedside clock told her to go back to sleep. The internal clock won the battle.

Stevie crept out of bed, pulled on a sweatshirt over her pajamas, and tiptoed out onto the bunkhouse porch, where she could sit on one of the aged deck chairs and look at the sky.

There was something very different about the night-time sky at The Bar None. At home, the sky was just a dark area with a few dim stars scattered here and there. Here, in the open country, without a sizable town for more than fifty miles, the sky was a rich black velvet sprinkled with thousands of bright stars, reaching from one end of the horizon to the other.

Although it was warm in the Southwest, it was late fall and the sun wouldn't be up for more than an hour. Until then, there was blackness, studded with brilliant pinpoints of light.

Stevie sighed. It was beautiful. It made her think of other country nights and other starry skies she'd seen. That, naturally, made her think of Phil Marston, her boyfriend. They didn't see each other very often because they lived about twenty minutes apart by car, but they talked on the phone a lot, and they'd be together again in the summer at camp, where they'd met in the first place. Stevie suddenly remembered that this trip had come up so fast she hadn't had time to tell Phil about it. She promised herself she'd get a postcard to send to him as soon as she and her friends could get to town.

Stevie leaned back in the deck chair and closed her eyes. She wasn't as wide-awake as she'd thought. She drifted toward sleep.

"Good morning." A voice awoke her.

Stevie sat up, startled. The sky was gray now, cloaking the world in its dim light. In front of her, a young girl was sitting bareback on a horse. Next to the horse, a half-grown puppy was gnawing playfully on a stick.

"Christine!" Stevie said, jumping up out of the chair and running to her friend. "How are you!"

Christine slid down off Arrow's back and greeted Stevie with a hug. "I'm fine, but what are you doing sleeping out on the porch at this hour? I mean, there are a thousand things to do. You going to sleep the day away?"

Stevie laughed. Christine Lonetree took an early-morning bareback ride every day. She always rode by The Bar None, and nobody had ever known it until Stevie had seen her on The Saddle Club's earlier visit to the ranch. When the girls became friends, Christine had taken them with her on her early-morning ride. It had been a very special ride, ending up at Christine's family's house across the valley from the ranch. Christine's mother had given them a wonderful pancake breakfast.

"Me, sleeping?" Stevie said innocently. "Why, I've already had my first ride of the day. I was just waiting to see if a lazybones like you would ever show up this morning."

"I can tell you've been up for hours, by the way you're rubbing your eyes and yawning," Christine teased. "And I love the riding duds. I ride in pajamas all the time."

Stevie laughed. "No fooling you, huh? Well, let's just get everybody else—" She turned to go into the cabin, but was stopped by something tugging insistently at the ankle of her pajamas. "What in . . ."

"Dude wants to say hello," Christine said, pointing

to the culprit, her curly-haired brown-and-white puppy.

Stevie remembered Dude well. In fact, she had been the one to give him to Christine. The last time she'd seen the puppy, he'd been little more than a sleepy, fuzzy ball. He'd grown a lot since then. He was full of energy, and appeared to have a great liking for pajama bottoms.

"He's so cute!" Stevie cooed, kneeling down and patting the energetic ball of fur. Dude turned his attention from Stevie's pajamas to her hand. He began licking it furiously. Then he jumped up on her and started licking at her ears.

"Down, Dude!" Christine said sharply. It didn't do any good at all. Stevie didn't mind, though. She was enjoying patting and hugging the puppy. After a few minutes, Dude discovered an oak leaf skittering across the porch. He growled protectively and then pounced at it.

"Time to wake everybody else up," Christine said. Stevie opened the cabin door for her and the two of them went in.

"Can you do reveille?" Stevie asked. Christine nodded. The two of them stood as if in formation and whistled the traditional "wake-up" song of camps and armies. It didn't work on their friends, so they resorted to a more direct method.

"Get out of bed, you lazybones! Look who's here!"

When Kate, Carole, and Lisa saw their visitor, they woke up immediately. Lisa and Carole hopped out of their bunks and ran to greet Christine. For a few minutes, there was a confusion of hugging, tooth brushing, and getting dressed. Within an amazingly short time, the five girls reassembled on the porch to visit until breakfast.

It turned out that Kate had called Christine to tell her the girls were arriving. Normally, Kate and Christine would have had school that week, but Christine explained that Saturday's rodeo was really a local festival and almost everybody in the area was participating in one way or another.

"They used to try to keep school open during Rodeo Week, but they found that nobody came. No teachers, no students. The principals in the district got together and threw in the towel."

"That's almost as much fun as burst pipes," Lisa said.

"Oh, I don't know," Kate remarked. "A planned vacation is never really as much fun as an unplanned one. I love the fact that you guys came on the spur of the moment, with nothing planned except the rodeo."

"Actually, there is something planned," Carole said. The other four girls looked at her in surprise. "It's something we talked about a while ago. We just never got to do it until now."

With that, Carole stood up and went into the cabin. Kate turned to Stevie for an explanation.

Stevie shrugged. "Beats me," she said.

"I think I know what she has in mind," Lisa said slowly. "And she's right. It's something we planned a very long time ago—the day we left here on our last trip."

Stevie thought back. And then she remembered.

"Here it is," Carole said, returning to the porch from the bunkroom, where she'd been rummaging around in her suitcase. She was holding something in her hand.

Lisa and Stevie arranged the chairs so the five girls sat in a circle. Then Carole spoke.

"Christine," she began, "as you may know, Stevie, Lisa, and I formed a group we call The Saddle Club. We only have two requirements for membership. Members must be horse crazy and members must be willing to help one another out. There's no doubt about it. You fit the bill perfectly. By unanimous vote, you've been elected to be a member. We hope you'll accept our offer and wear the pin proudly." Carole held out a small red jewelry box.

Christine didn't seem to know what to do. For a second, Stevie thought she might cry. But just then, Dude interfered. The puppy saw Carole's outstretched hand and assumed she wanted to pet him. He came bounding up to Carole and bounced into her, knocking the jewelry box into the air. Christine caught it.

Carole petted Dude while Christine opened the box. The early-morning sun glinted on the gift inside. The club pin was a silver horsehead. The horse's mane was brushed back by the wind, as if he were racing joyously.

"Oh," Christine gasped. "It's beautiful."

"Will you wear it?" Lisa asked.

"More important, will you join?" Stevie said.

"Of course I will! I'm proud to be a member of The Saddle Club. Are you in this, too?" she asked Kate.

"Yes, I am," Kate said. "You and I are now the western branch of the club. It's up to us to carry on Saddle Club traditions with a western flair. Think you're up to it?" Kate asked, grinning.

Solemnly, Christine crossed both arms out in front of her, and then raised her right arm from the elbow, holding her hand palm-forward. "How," she said, doing a convincing imitation of an old western-movie Indian.

Stevie burst into giggles. "Western is right! All the way to Hollywood! How corny can you get?"

Christine couldn't keep her straight face any longer. She started giggling as well.

"High twenty-five!" Carole said, holding up her hand. The five members of The Saddle Club all slapped hands together at once.

"Morning, girls," Eli greeted them as he walked by their cabin. He paused to pat Dude.

"Good morning," echoed Jeannie, who was trailing close behind Eli.

The girls returned the greetings.

"Eating breakfast today?" Eli asked while Jeannie patted the puppy.

Stevie half expected Jeannie to ask them that too.

"Tell Mom we'll be right there," Kate said, answering for them all. It was time to get ready for the day, whatever it would bring.

CAROLE HAD ALMOST forgotten about ranch breakfasts, until the courses started arriving. Phyllis Devine brought the steak and eggs first. Frank delivered the orange juice.

"Potatoes coming up!" Kate announced, pushing her way through the swinging door from the kitchen. Ranch breakfasts were serious food for serious appetites.

"This looks great!" Stevie remarked, reaching for the scrambled eggs. Kate and Lisa each helped themselves to potatoes. Eli started the steak platter around the long table.

It was a wonderful breakfast, except for one thing. There were only two paying guests in the entire dining room. The Bar None was a great guest ranch. Everything about it was terrific. Carole couldn't understand why it wouldn't be packed every night, but she could certainly understand that if it wasn't, it would be difficult to keep it running much longer.

"You want to, don't you?" Stevie asked Carole, interrupting her thoughts.

"Sure I do," Carole said without thinking. Then she added, "Er, what is it I just told you I want to do?"

Stevie grinned. "You want to go for a ride with Christine, don't you?"

"Oh, absolutely," Carole confirmed. She was getting the germ of a good idea, and a ride with Christine might be just exactly the way to carry it out. "As a matter of fact, the sooner the better. Let's go." She moved to stand up from the table.

"Don't you want to finish your breakfast first?" Phyllis asked.

"Or at least start it," Stevie said, looking at Carole's almost untouched plate.

Carole blushed. "Of course," she said. She picked up her fork and began eating. "I'm just being flaky again," she explained, though she had the feeling that it didn't require explanation. Everybody could tell she was being flaky. They just didn't know what she was being flaky about. That would have to wait until the next Saddle Club meeting. If she could get her friends to eat quickly, that meeting would take place in about fifteen minutes—on horseback!

"COME ON, GUYS. We've got to hurry," Carole said, standing up from the breakfast table. She stacked as many clean plates as she could reach—and some that weren't clean yet.

"Hold on!" Stevie said, a little annoyed when Carole tried to snatch her plate from her. "Just one more serving of potatoes, and—"

"You've had enough," Carole informed her. "Time to get going."

"Where's the fire?" Stevie asked, reluctantly relinquishing her plate.

"Right under our noses," Carole said mysteriously.

Stevie didn't have any idea what Carole was talking about, but when Carole got her mind onto something, there was no shaking it loose. She might as well give in. She stood up and joined the others in the kitchen.

"We'll have these dishes done in no time," Christine said.

"No need," Phyllis told the girls. "I'll take care of them this morning. You go on ahead, okay?"

Normally, Carole would have insisted that they all pitch in, but she was out the door before Phyllis finished her sentence. Stevie looked at Lisa. She was as puzzled as Stevie was. They shrugged and followed Carole out the door toward the corral.

Eli and Jeannie had rounded up a few horses for ranch use that day. The Bar None had a sizable herd to choose from and they tried to rotate the horses so each had equal riding time. However, it was also traditional for the guests to be assigned a horse for the duration of their stay.

"He remembered!" Stevie said, more than a little pleased to see that her horse from their earlier stay, Stewball, was standing quietly in the corral. A more careful inspection confirmed that Eli had remembered everybody's horse, for she also recognized Berry and Chocolate, the horses Carole and Lisa had ridden. Kate's horse, Spot, was also in the corral.

Eli grinned at her. "Sure I remembered," he said.

"You think I could forget the sight of you on that horse, taking a wily shortcut just so you could beat me to the creek that day?"

"Me? A shortcut?" Stevie asked innocently. "You think *I* would take advantage of *your* mistake just to beat you in a race?"

"Well,"—Eli drawled the word as if it were at least three syllables—"now that I recall, it was the horse that was smart enough to take a shortcut, not the rider."

Stevie started laughing then, and so did Eli. The fact was that he was absolutely right. That was why Stevie loved Stewball: He was fast and he was smart. She went over to him in the corral and gave him a hug. She could have sworn he remembered her.

It only took the girls a few minutes to saddle up. Western tack was bigger, heavier, and a bit more complicated to put on a horse than the English tack the girls used at Pine Hollow. They'd learned how to do it during their last visit and it didn't take long for the knowledge to come back.

"Let's go!" Carole urged her friends, mounting Berry and settling into the deep and comfortable saddle.

"Hold your horses!" Lisa said, a little annoyed. She giggled at the unintended joke. "I guess I mean that for real this time." Her friends laughed, too. Eli gave her a hand with the final adjustment of her horse's cinch and stirrups and they were off.

Carole led the group. When they'd gotten about

fifty yards out of the ranch complex, she drew Berry to a halt and waited for her friends to join her.

"We've got to talk," she said.

"Yeah, you going to tell us now what this is all about?" Stevie asked. "I mean, I don't see any fires out here, you know. So what's the hurry?"

"The hurry is saving The Bar None," Carole said. "That other ranch—what's it called again?"

"The Dapper Dude," Kate supplied.

"Right, The Dapper Dude is stealing business from The Bar None. If The Bar None doesn't put up a fight, the Devines will have to sell." Carole didn't say anything for a few seconds while everybody looked at Kate. She nodded, confirming their worst fears.

"Okay, so I know a few things about battles," Carole continued. "And the first thing to do when you go into battle is to know your enemy. We have to learn about The Dapper Dude."

"You mean we have to spy?" Lisa asked.

"That's exactly what I mean," Carole said. Her eyes lit up with excitement.

"Then shouldn't we be creeping around at night, dressed in desert camouflage or something?" Lisa asked.

"You've seen too many James Bond movies," Stevie teased.

"No, Lisa's right in a way," Carole said. "But the best camouflage lets you blend right in. So my plan is for us to mosey on over to The Dapper Dude in broad daylight and do just that."

"Aha!"

"Very clever!" Kate cried. "Then we can find out if they're doing anything we're not that we ought to be doing!"

"Wait a minute!" Christine said. "Is this one of those famous Saddle Club projects?" The girls told her it was. "So let me get this straight. You mean that being in The Saddle Club means sometimes we could get into trouble?" She looked serious.

"Only when it's necessary," Stevie told her. "Does that bother you? Do you want to drop out?"

Christine's face broke into a grin. "Drop out? No way!" she declared emphatically. "I *love* it! Let's go! I know a shortcut to The Dapper Dude!"

Christine gave her horse a kick. He broke into a lope. All the other horses followed immediately.

GETTING TO THE Dapper Dude was no trouble. It was just over a hill from The Bar None. Getting into it wasn't any trouble, either. The girls simply acted as though they belonged there. Everybody just assumed they were guests.

"Beginners' trail ride in fifteen minutes," one wrangler announced, trying to tempt them as they stood outside the main house. "You girls joining us?" Carole looked at what he was wearing. He was dressed like Eli or any other wrangler, in jeans, leather boots, a plaid shirt, and a wide-brimmed hat. But over his clothes, he wore a duster, which was a long black cotton coat, split up the back to the waist so it could be worn riding. It had a cape collar that would convert to a hood in the rain.

Lisa poked her in the arm, and Carole realized that she had to stop staring and answer his question. "No thanks, not today," she said firmly. The last thing she wanted was to get stuck on a trail ride going away from The Dapper Dude.

"We've got work to do here," Stevie explained

The wrangler looked at her as if she might just be a little bit crazy, but then shrugged his shoulders and moved on. There was a family standing on the porch with four young kids who seemed eager to go on the trail ride.

Carole gave Stevie a dirty look. "The less we say, the more we learn," she said. She was afraid that if Stevie's tongue got wagging, she'd give something away, like the reason they were all there.

Stevie grimaced and nodded. "Sorry, chief."

"First stop, the public areas," Kate said. "This is the main building. It's got to have the dining room and lounge areas and stuff like that."

"All dining rooms are the same," Lisa remarked. "What are we going to learn from that? We need to see the kitchen!"

"Who's going to show us the kitchen?" Christine wanted to know.

"The chef," Stevie said. "Come on." The Saddle Club hitched their horses up at the post outside the main building and entered, with Stevie in the lead.

The building was just what Kate had predicted and

was very much like The Bar None. The big difference was that every single table in the dining room was set for lunch, instead of just the staff table and one guest table, as at The Bar None.

"May I help you?" a young man asked the girls. Carole guessed he was the dining room manager. "Lunch won't be served for another hour and a half," he added.

"We're really hungry," Stevie said coaxingly. She smiled at him and blinked her eyes innocently.

It didn't work. "Like I said, an hour and a half," the man repeated.

"Couldn't we just pop into the kitchen and grab a little snack?" Stevie wheedled, ever the optimist.

"No need for that. You can have a full meal," the young man answered. "In an hour and a half." His politeness was definitely sounding strained.

Carole sensed that it was time to quit. "Thanks anyway," she said.

"Hmmm," the young man said. Carole noticed the absence of a "You're welcome."

The girls shuffled into the lounge, discouraged by their failure. The lounge was a large sitting room with coffee tables and game tables for cards and board games. It looked very much like the lounge at The Bar None.

Stevie started rummaging through the boxes of board games in the cabinet. "Monopoly . . . Candy Land . . . Chutes and Ladders . . . Life . . . Risk . . . Trivial Pursuit . . ."

As she named each game, Kate said, "Yup," confirming that The Bar None had the same selection.

". . . Pictionary."

"Hey, we don't have that one," Kate said excitedly. "But we can get it. I'm sure we can!"

"Oh, that'll make all the difference," Stevie said sarcastically.

"Probably not," Kate said. "See, we've got Clue and they don't."

Carole glanced at Kate to see if she seriously thought a couple of board games would make the difference between success and failure. The look on Kate's face told Carole that Kate knew better.

"Excuse me, miss," Lisa said, talking to a young woman who was tidying up the lounge. "Can you help me with something?"

"Sure," the housekeeper said agreeably. "If I can."

"Well, I've got this problem and I'm not having much luck convincing the guy who runs the dining room—you know, the guy with the icy stare?"

"Good old Rule-Book Marshall?"

"That's the one," Lisa said. "Anyway, I have this equine allergy and my doctor told me it would help if I made sure to have an, uh, well, you know, a glass of milk every morning at, uh"—she glanced at her watch—"eleven-seventeen. It's eleven-fifteen now and I'm going to start sneezing in exactly two minutes, but Marshall won't let me near the kitchen to get my milk. Can you help?"

The housekeeper's face began twitching oddly. Carole was afraid she was going to blow up. And she did, in a way. She exploded into laughter.

"You must really be desperate to think I'd fall for a story like that!" she said when her giggles subsided. "But anybody with that much imagination ought to be rewarded. Come with me."

Lisa didn't waste a second. She bounded after the housekeeper, following her through a door off the lounge into the sacred—and apparently secret—recesses of the ranch's kitchen.

Lisa emerged two minutes later, carrying a paper cup full of milk.

"So?" Kate asked.

"Other than the fact that it's painted white instead of yellow, it's about the same as your kitchen. Except that they're cooking chili for lunch and they've put in too many beans and not enough beef."

"I'm keeping a checklist, are you?" Stevie asked Christine.

Christine nodded. "So far, we've got to get the Devines to get rid of Clue, buy Pictionary, and add beans. Sounds to me like a formula for success."

"Don't forget about hiring a snobby dining room manager who makes the guests feel uncomfortable," Stevie suggested.

Carole scowled. She was beginning to think that their spying prank wasn't going to get them any useful information at all and she was annoyed at the failure. But she wasn't ready to give up yet.

"Come on, guys," she said. "There's something we're missing. I know there is." Her friends looked at her dubiously. Carole pursued the thought. "Look, a dude ranch isn't successful because of board games and beans. It's the horses and the riding program that matter. So what are we doing here in the lounge? Let's get to the stable!"

The other girls agreed that it couldn't hurt to take a look. They unhitched their horses and walked them over to the corral, which bordered the stable. The corral contained all the horses that had been rounded up for the guests for the day. It was just the same as the corral at The Bar None.

"The horses all look fine," Kate said, observing them carefully. Carole had to agree with her friend. All the animals appeared to be healthy and well taken care of. Some pranced around the corral, while others stood quietly. It was a normal mix of horses. There probably weren't any prizewinners in the corral, but there weren't any flea-bitten nags, either.

"You're right," Carole told Kate. "Nothing unusual here. Your horses are just as good."

"Tack," Stevie said suddenly. "Tack's really important. We've got to get to the tack room."

"Just like we had to get to the kitchen?" Lisa asked, reminding Stevie that so far their mission hadn't exactly been a screaming success.

"It's worth trying," Stevie countered. Nobody could disagree with that. "Now, let's see," she said, thinking out loud. "I need to find a wrangler and tell him about this allergy I have . . ." She looked out of the corner of her eye at Lisa, who blushed.

"All right, I'm not as good as you," Lisa said, sounding a little defensive. "I know you would have come up with something better. But it worked, didn't it?"

"What worked?" a man asked, approaching them from inside the corral. He was one of the ranch wranglers, dressed in what seemed to be the wranglers' uniform of jeans, plaid shirt, and hat. He was also wearing a black duster. Carole liked the dusters. She wondered if she could wear one, then decided it wouldn't look right over her English riding togs.

"My friend here has really bad allergies. She was saying that her medicine worked," Stevie told the man, keeping a straight face.

The wrangler looked at them patronizingly. "Not a real good idea to hang around too close to the corral," he warned them. "The horses could nip you or something. We wouldn't want you to get hurt."

"We can take care of ourselves," Stevie retorted.

"Oh, good," he said. "So what are you doing hanging around here? Why aren't you on the trail ride with the other dudes?"

Carole suspected Christine was adding condescending, rude wranglers to the list of things The Bar None would have to get to compete with The Dapper Dude.

"It just so happens that I have a problem with my tack," Stevie told the wrangler.

"You do? And what might that be?" he asked.

Everybody looked at Stevie, especially Lisa. She

wanted to see if Stevie could come up with a more believable whopper than hers.

Stevie's voice took on a spoiled, whining tone. "See, there's this sort of smudged place on the saddle and I'm awfully afraid that it's going to get my jeans dirty. Isn't there some sort of soap or something you could use to clean it up? Or could I have a new saddle?"

The girls held their breath. The wrangler looked at Stevie closely. Carole had the feeling that it was going to work. The look on the man's face clearly indicated that a dumb remark like that was just about what he would expect from a greenhorn like Stevie. Carole especially liked the part Stevie had added about "something you could use to clean it up." She knew this wrangler wouldn't be caught dead soaping a saddle for the kind of dumb dude Stevie was pretending to be.

"We've got just the thing for you, miss," he said, very politely now. "It's called saddle soap. I'll show you where it is. You can do the cleaning yourself. After all, I wouldn't want to leave any dusty residue on the saddle that might soil those nice clean jeans of yours. This way, please."

Stevie followed him. Before she entered the barn, she turned back to her friends and winked. Lisa gave her a thumbs-up signal.

"Just forty-five minutes now until lunch," came a familiar, unwelcome voice from behind them. It was Rule-Book Marshall. He walked past them quickly and officiously.

"Gee, thanks," Carole called after him.

Stevie emerged from the stable with some saddle soap on a paper towel. She was about to toss it aside, but Carole made her use it on Stewball's saddle.

"What if somebody's watching?" Carole asked. "They'll know that was just a fib."

Stevie rubbed the soap into the seat of the saddle. "That was much too believable for anybody to suspect," she said, teasing Lisa as she spoke.

"I believed it." Lisa smiled ruefully. "It sounded to me as if you were quoting Veronica diAngelo!" Veronica was an overrich, overindulged rider at Pine Hollow who believed that the sole function of all the stablehands there was to help her.

"I was," Stevie said. Lisa could believe that, too.

Stevie finished the soaping and put the paper towel into the garbage. "Well, guys, the tack room here is just a tack room. No silver bridles to lure the tourists. Just leather, dust, and cobwebs."

"What's next?" Christine asked. Carole shook her head. She didn't know what to do next.

"Hey, Lisa, how's the sneezing going?" somebody called out. The girls looked up. It was the housekeeper who had sneaked Lisa into the kitchen.

"Fine, thanks," Lisa replied, somewhat flustered.

"That's it," Carole decided. "It's time to go. We've stopped blending in and have started to stand out. We'll be discovered it we stick around for two more minutes. Let's go!"

The girls mounted and began riding toward the ranch's gate.

"Stand out?" Stevie said, as if the thought hadn't occurred to her. "But we never even had a chance to explain about the tour group of reform-school refugees we wanted to bring, so we would need a tour of all the guest rooms. And I just know the reason I didn't have good hot water this morning was because the boiler must be broken and I'd know just what to do if I could get a look at it. Oh! And the root cellar! I bet their vegetables don't hold a candle to my dad's prize parsnips . . ."

"Uncle! Uncle! I give up!" Lisa declared as they passed under the sign welcoming guests to The Dapper Dude. "You can tell better stories than I can. You have always told better stories than any of us. You win the crown!"

"Oh, I don't know about that," Christine said. "After all, I didn't even have a chance to explain how I heard a rumor that President Reagan stayed here and I wanted to see all of their guest books to look at his autograph."

"What about me?" Kate said. "I'm an amateur entomologist and I need to check out the spiders in the attic."

"Right," Lisa said. "Now get this: We're actually government agents and we heard of this spy ring disguised as wranglers. . . ."

The girls chattered on, giggling at the most outrageous yarns. Carole laughed with them, but she was thinking as well. They hadn't seen all of the rooms, the guest book, or the attic at The Dapper Dude, but it seemed clear that it was a guest ranch just the same as The Bar None. So why was it succeeding when The Bar None was failing?

"WHERE ARE WE going?" Stevie asked Kate, who was in the lead.

"We're going into town," Kate said. "It's only another couple of miles past The Dapper Dude. I figured since we'd be too late for lunch at home and we certainly didn't want to test the hospitality at The Dapper Dude any more, we ought to buy ourselves something in Two Mile Creek."

"Something really nutritious, like what we got at the ice cream place the last time we were there?" Stevie asked.

"Something like that." Kate laughed. "They do have hamburgers and salads there, too."

Stevie remembered their last visit to the town. There was a cowboy show in the main street every afternoon. At three o'clock sharp, bank robbers had shown up to steal the payroll and shortly thereafter, the marshal and his posse had arrived to put them all behind bars. A shoot-out had ensued. Stevie had really had a wonderful time at the show. In fact, she'd actually believed it was true. It didn't occur to her at first that real bad guys probably wouldn't be wearing microphones to amplify their voices—or, in the late twentieth century, make their getaways on horseback. She'd swallowed the whole thing, hook, line, and sinker, until the audience had started applauding.

Naturally, Stevie had never told Carole and Lisa that she'd been taken in. There were things she could tell her best friends and there were things she thought she should just keep to herself. That episode was in the latter category. Still, she had enjoyed the show and she hoped they'd be in town long enough today to see it again.

Stevie realized then that Kate had changed the subject. She began listening. "You know, I don't think their success has anything to do with being any better than The Bar None. They're not," Kate was saying. "They're just doing a better job than we are about tooting their own horn. Only a few people around here know about The Bar None. Everybody knows about The Dapper Dude."

"So we wasted our time snooping?" Lisa asked.

"Oh, no, not at all," Kate said. "That was an important thing to learn. And besides, we did learn about Pictionary!" The girls laughed. Then Kate stopped her horse.

"Look! There it is!" she said.

The Saddle Club looked where she was pointing. A quarter of a mile ahead of them lay the town of Two Mile Creek. It was little more than a main street, appropriately called Main Street, and a few side streets. But it looked different from the last time they had seen it. On the north side of town, the rodeo had been set up. There was a large grandstand, a number of tents, and corrals. Red, white, and blue banners and bunting decorated half of the structures. The rest apparently had yet to be done.

"Doesn't the arena look wonderful?" Kate asked, almost breathlessly.

Stevie glanced at Kate. It was odd that she should say that, because that was exactly the same way Stevie felt. But Kate had been a national championship rider, competing in the most prestigious horse shows in the country. She must have seen hundreds of horse shows set up in fields. Why would this be any different? What would make it wonderful? There was only one possible answer: It was *rodeo*.

Rodeos were different. They weren't the stylized, elegant riding of perfectly groomed horses, manicured hooves, or polished saddles, with horses flying effortlessly over jumps, or showing off their perfect gaits around a ring in a preset pattern. Rodeo was wild and dusty and fast and furious. It was bronco bucking, bull riding, rope twirling, hell-bent-for-leather excitement and romance rolled into one. Stevie's heart beat faster at the thought.

"Let's go!" she cried out to her friends. And, following her lead, they all galloped toward the town.

They had to cool down their horses before they could go to the restaurant. It was a good chance to get a closer look at the rodeo, and they had their horses circle it at a walk.

Some workers were assembling the final seats in the grandstand, while others completed the bunting. A few horses eyed their activity skeptically from one of the temporary corrals. Everywhere Stevie looked, something was going on.

All these strangers were working busily at one thing or another. Then it turned out that not all of them were strangers.

"Hi there, dudes!"

It was Eli. He was just coming out of a tent. A lot of wranglers seemed to be standing in a line ouside it waiting to go in.

"What are *you* doing here?" Stevie asked.

"I just registered for my events," he explained. "I'm heading back to the ranch now. I'll see you girls later."

He waved cheerfully and left them by the line of rodeo cowboys.

Stevie looked over the crowd. The young men who were lined up looked strong and healthy and outdoorsy. They were tanned from the strong south-western sun. They seemed to come in all sizes and shapes. Stevie realized with a start that there were girls their own age on the line with the men.

"What are those girls doing there?" Stevie blurted out. "I mean, I'm all in favor of equality, but I can't see a girl doing any steer wrestling!"

There was loud guffawing in response to her question. Stevie hadn't meant the question to be heard by everybody, but her surprise had made her talk louder than she'd intended.

"Those are the barrel-racing teams," one of the cowboys informed her.

Stevie looked at her friends. They seemed as embarrassed as she was.

She walked Stewball over closer to the cowboy who had spoken, so the whole world wouldn't listen in on her next question. "You mean girls compete in the rodeo, too?"

The cowboy nodded. "Yep," he said. "At this rodeo, it's an under-eighteen event, too, as you may be able to tell."

Stevie had the sneaking suspicion that he was trying not to laugh. She didn't care, much.

"Hmmm," Stevie mused.

"Come on, guys. I'm starving," Kate said. "Let's get some food."

Stevie's mind began to race, and she knew what that meant. First, when it began with an idea there was no stopping it. And second, when it stopped, there was no telling what she would end up doing.

"Uh, wait up a second," Stevie said. "I just got an idea."

She and Stewball rejoined the group.

Carole recognized the look in Stevie's eye. Sometimes it meant trouble, but it also meant fun. "Is this a Saddle Club meeting?" she asked.

Stevie nodded. Carole thought she knew what was coming. She glanced at the others. It looked like they all knew what Stevie was thinking. Wordlessly, the five girls formed a circle so they could talk in some privacy.

"I didn't know, did you?" Stevie asked Kate.

"I've never been to a rodeo before," Kate told her.

"Me, neither," Christine admitted. "After all, my ancestors weren't the cowboys." The girls giggled at Christine's joke.

"So?" Stevie asked.

"I say we do it," Carole stated, casting her vote.

"Me, too," Lisa agreed, and Kate and Christine added their approval.

"Then it's unanimous!" Stevie exclaimed. "Let's go!"

FOOD WAS DELAYED for a half hour while The Saddle Club registered for the barrel-racing event in the rodeo.

"Name?" the woman behind the desk asked.

"Stephanie, but I'm called Stevie," she answered promptly. "And this is . . ."

"Not your name, your *team* name," the woman said,

more sharply than Stevie thought was necessary. She suspected the woman thought they ought to be called The Fools.

Stevie looked at her friends. The obvious answer was The Saddle Club, but that wasn't quite right. They were doing this to have fun, of course, but mostly, they wanted to help publicize The Bar None.

Stevie snapped her fingers. "The Bar None Riders!" she answered. Smiles from her friends confirmed their approval.

"Twenty-five dollars, please," the woman said. The girls looked at each other. This, they hadn't expected.

"Money?" Stevie said, realizing afterward how dumb the question sounded.

The woman nodded.

The girls dug down into their pockets and pooled their resources. Stevie could see people behind them in the line snickering.

Bills and coins appeared on the desk. Lisa, the straight-A student, took charge of counting up the cash. "Twenty-four dollars and eighty-three cents," she announced at last.

The woman at the table shook her head. "Twenty-*five* dollars," she reminded the girls, as if they needed reminding.

"Can we owe it to you?" Stevie asked. Since her usual cash position was negative, she was used to owing people money.

"Twenty-five dollars," the woman said steadily.

"Here you go, girls," the cowboy behind them said,

putting seventeen cents on the table. "I'm more than pleased to contribute to your team. I wouldn't miss your performance in the ring for anything—if your performance in the registration tent is any indication of things to come!"

Everybody within earshot hooted with laughter. Stevie could feel herself blushing from head to toe. The woman behind the desk just counted the money.

"Here are your numbers and your instructions," she said when she'd put the cash in her strong box. She gave the package to Christine.

They were in!

LUNCH WAS OUT of the question, since they'd spent every penny they had on entering the rodeo. The rodeo supplied some hay and water for their horses, but nothing for the girls. Stomachs growling, they walked their horses back out of town toward The Bar None.

"This is so exciting!" Lisa exclaimed.

"Imagine, the first rodeo we've ever been to and we're even going to be *in* it!" Carole exulted.

"Well, according to this stuff from the package, we're even going to be in the rodeo parade," Christine told them, looking up from a booklet.

"Wow!" Lisa said.

"Aren't you excited?" Kate asked Stevie. "I mean, you look so serious."

"Oh, sure I'm excited," Stevie said. "Who wouldn't be? Only, there are two things bothering me."

"So, what are they?" Carole asked.

"Well, first, we want to do our best anyway, but since we're called The Bar None Riders, our best has to be *the* best."

"Of course," Kate said. "We all know that. So what's the second thing on your mind?"

"This one's a little trickier," Stevie said. She hesitated, stalling for time. Her friends waited expectantly. Finally, she blurted it out.

"What's barrel racing?"

"I MEAN, REALLY, how do you race barrels?" Stevie
asked.

The five girls were seated around the cook's table in
the kitchen at The Bar None, munching on cold
chicken, which Kate had found in the refrigerator.
The chicken tasted wonderful, although they were so
hungry by then that they would have eaten cactus!

"Maybe one person rolls it and another rides on
horseback and races the roller?" Lisa suggested. "Nah,
that's stupid," she said, answering her own question
before her friends answered it for her.

"Some kind of relay race?" Carole said.

"Probably," Kate agreed. "After all, we're a team. Teams do relay races."

"We're good at relay races," Stevie said. "Remember the gymkhana?"

They all remembered it well, and they told Christine about it. With Kate's help, The Saddle Club had come in first in the gymkhana at Pine Hollow's horse show in the summer.

"But somehow, I don't think a barrel race will involve squirt guns and clown costumes," Kate remarked.

"Well, there must be something here. . . ." Christine thumbed through the material they'd gotten at registration. "Ah! Here it is. It says: 'Barrel-racing teams will be judged on performance as a whole, competing against all other teams. The final score will be the total of the four best scores on the team. In addition to a winning team, the single best score of the event will receive an individual event championship prize.'"

"Good," Lisa said. "So if I blow it, it won't hurt you guys—or The Bar None."

"Nobody's going to blow it," Carole assured her. "But we still don't know what 'it' is."

Then somebody came to their rescue. It was Eli, coming in from the barn.

"Gosh, I'm hungry," he declared as he entered the kitchen and washed his hands at the sink.

"We'll share our chicken if you'll share information," Stevie said, holding a chicken leg in front of him tantalizingly.

Kate lifted a bowl of chips and fanned the wonderful greasy potato odor toward his nose to tempt him. "All this could be yours," she said, sounding like an announcer on a game show. "Plus a glass of milk—if you know the answer!"

Eli took off his hat and pulled up a chair. "For lunch, I'll tell you anything."

"*And* promise not to laugh at us," Stevie said solemnly.

Eli pushed his chair back from the table and began to stand up. "That's more 'n ah kin guarantee," he said, exaggerating his western drawl. "Sometahmes ah jes' cain't hep layfin' at the antics of *dudes*."

"Come on, guys. We're at his mercy," Lisa said. "What have we got to lose?"

"You mean he's got us over a barrel race?" Stevie suggested. Her friends groaned at the pun.

Eli sat down again. Christine produced a plate. Lisa handed him a napkin. Stevie gave him some chicken. Kate put potato chips on his plate. Carole poured the milk and spoke for them all.

"What's barrel racing?" she asked.

Eli stopped eating and looked at the girls strangely. "I'd be glad to tell you all about it," he said. "Why would you think I'd laugh at you for not knowing about it? I know you don't know anything about rodeos. Why should I expect you to know anything about barrel racing?" He took a drink of milk.

Everybody looked at Stevie to answer that one. After all, it had been her idea in the first place. Stevie cleared her throat. "Because we haven't told you the best part yet. You're having lunch with The Bar None Riders, officially registered for barrel racing in the Two Mile Creek Rodeo."

For a second, Eli just looked at the five girls. Then it happened, just like they'd thought it would. Eli's shoulders began shaking. His face reddened as he fought to swallow the milk before the laughter took over his whole body. Finally, when the milk was safely downed, he began roaring.

Kate put her hands on her hips. "You promised!" she said. "And besides, what's so funny?"

Eli's laughter subsided. "Oh, nothin'," he said, wiping his eyes. "Nothin's funny. It's just that—" He was about to laugh some more, but controlled it this time.

"I don't think it's so strange that you should want to try your hands at barrel racing," Eli sputtered. "As a matter of fact, you'll probably do okay. I just think it's funny that you'd sign up for it without . . . without . . . I mean before . . ."

"Stop laughing and tell us what it is," Stevie commanded in her best no-nonsense-manner.

Eli caught his breath and began. "It's a race around three barrels. They're in a big triangle. When the bell sounds, you gallop straight into the ring, so you've got one barrel to your right, one to the left, and one straight ahead. You make a sharp right and do a right turn around the first barrel, head back to the one that was to your left, make a left turn around that, go for the far barrel, circle that left and return to the starting line."

"Wow! That's simple!" Stevie said brightly.

"Doing the event's easy. Winning it is hard," Eli said, correcting her. "Now that's all the time I've got for chitchat," he said, pushing his chair back. "I've got some more practicing to do." He put on his hat, touched his brim to bid the girls good-bye, and left the kitchen.

"Maybe we should practice, too," Christine suggested.

"Couldn't hurt," Stevie added.

"YEOUCH!" STEVIE HOWLED a half hour later. Practice, it turned out, could hurt a lot! She had just flown out of Stewball's saddle and landed unceremoniously on her backside. "Watch out for the corners, guys!"

It was Stevie's third try at the barrels. Just as Eli had said, it *was* easy—to be bad at.

"Don't go so fast around the corners," Lisa suggested.

"But you have to go fast around the corners," Kate argued. "The trick isn't to slow down. It's to stay on going fast."

Stevie held Stewball's reins and walked over to the corral fence where her friends waited. "Your turn," she told Christine.

"Don't you want to try again?" Christine asked,

grinning. "I mean, you know about how important it is to get back on the horse and all, don't you?"

"Yeah, I know it," Stevie said, rubbing the part of her where she'd landed. "But I think I'll sit out, or should I say *stand* out for a few minutes—get it?"

"I get it." Christine climbed onto the blanket on Arrow's back. She was used to riding bareback. She was sure it would be okay for barrel racing. But it wasn't. This time, instead of just the rider ending in the dirt, the rider *and* her blanket ended in the dirt.

"You try it, Kate," Christine said, joining Stevie at the sideline.

Kate was the undisputed best rider of the bunch. Carole thought that if anybody had a chance, Kate did. All the girls watched closely, hoping whatever she did would work and they could learn from it.

"I'm going to approach this scientifically," Kate told her friends.

"Just the way I did," Stevie said. "Going ballistic is very scientific!" Everybody laughed. It was good for them to laugh right then because, although nobody wanted to admit it, things were looking pretty bleak for The Bar None Riders.

First Kate walked through the entire course, much the same way a competitor might do before an important jumping event.

"She's pacing the thing out," Carole observed. "What a great idea."

"What do you mean?" Lisa asked.

"It's always helpful for you and the horse to know how many strides a course is. It's a way of measuring the distance between jumps so a rider knows how many steps her horse will need between them. Here, though, Kate wants to know when to start signaling for those turns. Those are very sharp turns and the horse is going to have to change leads as he comes out of them. Kate's not only being scientific, she's being smart."

Lisa watched more carefully. At a canter, or a lope, as the western riders called it, a horse could lead, or reach out, with either front leg. As long as the horse was going straight, it didn't matter which leg he used. But when the horse was circling something, the inside leg had to lead, and support his weight. Otherwise the horse would become unbalanced, the gait would be unsteady, and the rider was more likely to fly off, especially on a sharp turn.

Next, Kate mounted Spot and walked the course with him. What Kate was doing made sense to Lisa, but something bothered her. "Aren't we going to have to do this at a gallop?" she asked Carole.

"Maybe, one day," Carole said. "Right now, though, I think we'll be lucky if one of us gets through this and stays in the saddle!"

Lisa watched even more carefully.

Kate's horse, Spot, was an Appaloosa, and had been bred for fast starts, stops, and turns, all important qualities in cowboy horses, since they were traditionally used to cut cattle from herds. Once Spot and Kate had been around the course slowly a few times, he seemed to understand what he was supposed to do. So did she. Each time Kate did the course, she went a little faster. But her progress still seemed so slow!

At first, she and Spot did it at a slow walk. Then they moved through it at a more collected walk, then an extended walk. Lisa hoped very much that one day she would have the ability to control her horse's gait the way Kate could. For now, as somebody who was still a fairly new rider, she always felt fortunate to have the horse performing the basic gait she wanted at all.

Kate moved up to a trot. It seemed smooth and sleek to Lisa. Certainly, it wasn't fast enough to win any prizes, but it looked good.

"Now she's going to canter!" Carole said, the excitement rising in her voice.

Lisa watched while Kate cantered the course three times, each time going progressively faster. It looked great and she stayed on her horse.

"What are you all up to?" Jeannie Sanders asked, joining the watchers at the corral fence.

"We're watching Kate train to be a championship barrel racer," Lisa said proudly.

"Yeah, we want to take the prize at the rodeo to show people what a great ranch this is, so we can start taking business away from The Dapper Dude," Stevie added.

"It's a nice idea, but you're not going to take any prizes riding like that!" Jeannie said.

Lisa knew they had a long way to go, but she was annoyed at Jeannie's tone of voice. "And you think you can do it better?" she asked.

"Yeah, I do," Jeannie said matter-of-factly.

Kate completed the course, brought Spot over to the fence, and dismounted, obviously pleased with her progress. The Saddle Club members patted her on the back to congratulate her.

"Jeannie thinks she can do better than you," Lisa said. "So why don't you lend her your horse, since he's warmed up."

"Be my guest," Kate said, handing her the reins.

Jeannie mounted Spot, turned him to face the triangle and, on a signal from Kate, whacked Spot on the flank and simultaneously spurred him into a gallop. The girls couldn't believe what they were seeing! Jeannie had Spot at a flat-out gallop through the entire course, only slowing a little bit to circle the barrels. At each turn, Spot nearly brushed the barrel—once, it even tottered a bit—but he didn't knock one down. Then, almost before the girls knew what was happening, Jeannie drew Spot to a screeching straight-legged halt right in front of them, spraying dirt behind her. She'd completed the course in about one-third of the time Kate had done it at a canter.

"I guess we have a lot of work to do, don't we?" Kate asked, humbled by the sight she'd just seen.

"Yeah, but I'll help you," Jeannie said. "Now, it's time to rest your horses and, I suspect, your bruised backsides. Come on over to the north corral and watch Eli. He could use some cheering, too."

"STEER WRESTLING IS the roughest event for Eli,"

Jeannie explained on their way over to the corral. "It takes brute strength. He's got that, all right, but he's not heavy himself. It doesn't take much effort on the steer's part to haul him around a bit. And that costs precious seconds!"

The girls all climbed up onto the split-rail fence to watch. On a signal from Jeannie, Eli and another wrangler, named Jeff, galloped out of the starting gate with a steer just ahead of Eli. Quickly, Eli edged toward the steer, leaned down off his horse, grabbed the steer by its horns with his arms, slid off his horse, and forced the steer onto its side. It was something to watch!

"Yahoo!" Jeannie cried. "That was perfect!" The girls cheered wildly with her. Jeff rounded up the loose steer and brought him back into the barn while Eli came over to talk to his audience.

"That's the first time I've done it right," Eli said. "I'm telling you, that steer has spent so much time running wild in this corral that I think he just got tuckered out. So, working with a steer that's got some life in him is just one of my problems."

"What's the other?" Carole asked.

"Jeff. He's a really good hazer, but he's not going to be in town for the weekend so he can't haze for me when I'll need him the most. I've got to get to town and find another cowboy to haze for me at the rodeo."

"What's so important about hazing?" Stevie wanted to know.

"Your hazer's your partner," Eli explained. "If he's

good at keeping the steer running in a straight line—and he should be—he can be the difference between whether you win or if you let the clock run out just ·trying to find the darned animal in the corral."

"I—uh—Eli—" Jeannie began hesitantly. Eli looked at her patiently. "Um, well—you really did a good job. And, and you'll do fine on Saturday. I'm sure of it."

Lisa couldn't help thinking that that wasn't what Jeannie meant to say when she started talking. But it was clear she wasn't going to say any more right then. Her face had settled into the look of awed adoration that Eli hadn't noticed in the first place and didn't seem about to start noticing right then. He was all business when it came to rodeos.

"Now, I've got to try to work on my roping," he said. "You girls want to be moving targets for me?"

In their most unified act of the day, the girls said "No," in a single voice.

THE EVENING WAS still and quiet. As far as Lisa could see in the twilight desert, all the world was open space, mountains, and sky. There was no wind. It was still, silent.

"When I see a place like this, it always makes me wonder why man invented civilization," Lisa remarked.

"So somebody would have the opportunity to come up with a recipe for marshmallows, because they are absolutely critical to s'mores," Stevie informed her.

"So's a fire and we haven't had much luck with that," Lisa countered.

All five of the girls were sitting at a campsite on a hillside near a cave. The horses were bedded down for the night by the creek at the bottom of the hill. It had taken a lot of begging, and not a few phone calls, to get permission to ride to this campsite to spend the night. As far as Lisa was concerned, if absolutely nothing else went right during their whole trip, this, at least, was as it should be.

"Come on, I'll show you how to get a fire going," Christine said. She began piling dry wood and brush in the fireplace that had been used by previous campers.

"Is this an old Indian way?" Stevie asked.

"Only if you think using newspapers and a butane lighter constitute tribal customs."

Stevie laughed. She remembered how she had expected Christine to be like Indians she'd seen in movies, involved with mysterious rituals, hidden treasures, and that sort of thing. That was before the girls had gotten to know each other. Once they'd become friends, Stevie realized how dumb those expectations had been. Christine was a modern American girl, just like Stevie was. Now that she knew better, Stevie and Christine sometimes joked about it. Stevie knew, however, that Christine wouldn't think the jokes were funny if Stevie didn't know better. Only close friends could joke about important things. Christine's Native American heritage was important.

"Here we go," Christine said, lighting the papers. Soon the fire was glowing brightly and burning well. The large logs on top of the kindling crackled, confirming that the fire was now safely lit.

Stevie speared a marshmallow with a stick and held it toward the campfire.

"Dinner first!" Lisa protested, a little appalled that Stevie would be eating s'mores before hamburgers.

Stevie shook her head in disagreement. "I have a new motto," she said. "It goes like this: 'Life is uncertain—eat dessert first!'"

"Well," Lisa said, "if you put it that way—" She, too, took a long stick and pierced a marshmallow. After all, she told herself, they were on a camping trip, not a nutrition trip.

Soon, five marshmallows were toasting in the fire.

"I found an open space where we can practice tomorrow," Kate said.

Carole leaned forward to look closely to check her marshmallow. "But what are we going to do for barrels?" she asked.

"We don't need them in this place," Kate said. "See, it's completely open except for three big spiny cactus plants. Those big prickles will keep us from riding too close. It'll be perfect!"

"If only our riding could be!" Lisa groaned. "We have so much work to do. It didn't seem like we were so bad—until Jeannie showed us how good we'd need to be!"

"Perfect!" Stevie declared, admiring the golden-brown marshmallow on her stick. Deftly, she slid it off the stick onto the square of chocolate and sandwiched them between two graham crackers.

Christine talked while she assembled her s'more. "You ever hear the one about the guy who arrived in town the day of the big rodeo?" she asked her friends. They shook their heads. "Well, seems he hailed a cab at the airport. He climbed into the backseat and he said to the driver, 'Can you tell me how to get to the rodeo?' The cab driver said, 'Sure. Practice, practice, *practice!*'"

Stevie giggled. "That's not bad. I'll have to tell that one to Colonel Hanson."

Carole rolled her eyes. Stevie and her father loved swapping corny jokes.

"Just a minute," Lisa said sensibly. "This is a sort of Saddle Club meeting. Let's not talk about jokes. Let's talk about horses. I wanted to ask you about something I noticed today while I was riding Chocolate."

"What's that?" Carole asked. Lisa knew she would be interested. After all, nothing made Carole happier than sharing information about horses and riding.

"Well, she seems like she's almost a different horse when she's leading a group from when she's in the middle or at the end of it. Why is that?"

"It's true of a lot of horses," Carole said. "And it's one of the things that sometimes makes it hard to ride on trails with groups. A horse in the middle of a pack is going to be influenced by the horse right in front of it. That's partly because it's likely the horse feels some sort of competitive spirit with the horse in front. Part of it is that they take signals from the front, too, so if the horse in the lead begins the canter, the ones behind will follow, even before riders ask for it."

"I've noticed," Lisa said, "and I don't like it. I like to be the one to tell my horse what to do."

"Absolutely," Kate agreed. "You have to be. Otherwise, the horse will just stop paying attention to you. There are a couple of tricks I learned that might help you with that. The best I found was to keep a fairly tight rein and to keep it moving—just a tiny bit. What I mean is that even when nothing else is going on, you wiggle the rein slightly. It's like the start of a signal, but without a message. It doesn't tell the horse anything; it just gets his attention."

"That makes sense," Lisa said. "I'll try it."

"It won't stop Chocolate from *wanting* to play follow-the-leader with the other horse. It'll just keep her from doing it," Stevie added.

"You know what I've been wondering," Christine asked, "is how I can get some cowboy boots to wear in the parade on Saturday. I've outgrown the ones I have."

"We've got a whole lot of them at the ranch to lend to guests. You can take your pick," Kate offered.

"That would be great. Thanks." Christine smiled.

"So, now that we've taken care of Christine's feet, what are we going to wear on the rest of our bodies?" Stevie asked.

"Hey, she's right!" Lisa said. "A parade's a parade!

We can't go just wearing jeans and plaid shirts, can we?"

"No, I think we also ought to wear socks, and hats—"

"Very funny, Stevie," Lisa said.

The girls talked about that for a long time. The only conclusion they could come to was that they ought to wear something special for the parade.

"After all, we need to look like a *team*," Lisa declared.

"A team of what, though—that's the question," Stevie remarked.

"A team of winners," Carole said firmly, leaving no doubt in anyone's mind about Carole's determination. "We'll practice; we'll win. It'll be good for the rodeo, good for us, and most of all, good for The Bar None."

"What exactly is the prize?" Stevie asked.

"Five hundred dollars," Christine said. "And the individual winner gets one hundred."

"Wow! That's six hundred dollars! We can have a blast with that! Let me see—" Stevie began calculating out loud. "That's a hundred and twenty apiece or, really, one hundred each except for Kate, who would get two hundred—"

"Wait a minute," Kate said. "There's no guarantee I'd win the individual—"

"But you're the most experienced rider among us," Carole reasoned.

"That doesn't make me a rodeo champ. But anyway,

I'm in this for The Bar None, so if I win anything the money is going to the ranch."

Lisa smiled. It was right. Just plain right. She looked at her friends to see what they thought. They all liked the idea.

"That would buy a lot of shingles and paint," Kate said. "It would pay for the new toilet we need in Cabin Four. It might even buy some new tack for the horses, or a new tent for the round ups."

"And a game of Pictionary?" Stevie added.

The girls laughed.

"Well, count me in on that," Carole said, more seriously now. "Anything I win goes to the ranch, too."

"Me, too," Lisa said.

"Me, three," Christine added.

"Since that's why we're in this, it's the way that makes sense," Stevie agreed.

The girls finished up their dinner, cleaned after themselves, and got into their sleeping bags. They weren't tired yet, but the desert night was becoming cool. They could talk bundled snugly in their sleeping bags as well as they could sitting up and freezing, so that was what they did. They talked for hours on their favorite subject, horses.

When the talk had quieted down and the girls were ready to sleep, Lisa once again found herself gazing at the sky, now a deep black. She imagined she was riding a path through the stars on horseback, weaving and circling, flying with the clouds. Her horse seemed to anticipate her every command, turning faster than she could signal, going through the path at the speed of the wind. She never made a mistake. She never fell off.

Lisa drifted to sleep, dreaming of victory, glory, honor, shingles, toilets, Pictionary, and full bunkhouses. They would win. They had to win.

"HOLD WITH YOUR legs! Grip with your thighs!" Christine yelled at Stevie the next morning. Stevie held on for dear life. Stewball had just been bitten by the racing bug and he was running his heart out on the cactus race course that Kate had found for them.

Stevie could feel herself lose her balance as Stewball rounded the second cactus. The last thing she wanted was to be dumped on the hard desert. There were rocks, cacti, and snakes down there! She gripped harder, shifted her weight ever so slightly, and regained her equilibrium. Stewball galloped to the final cactus, circled it, and raced back to the finish line, where he came to a straight-legged halt.

"*Outstanding!*" Kate said, clapping Stevie on the back. "What was her time?"

Christine checked her watch. "Thirty-two seconds," Christine said. "That's almost a full fifteen seconds better than your last time, but you went around the final cactus the wrong way. It's a left-hand turn, not right!"

"There's instant penalty points for me. I can hear it

now. 'Congratulations, you were the fastest, but you lost. . . .'"

"Right, left, left. Right, left, left," Lisa said out loud. "I think I've got it."

"All right, then it's your turn," Christine said, resetting the stopwatch.

Lisa mounted Chocolate. The horse shifted uneasily, as if she were about to do something naughty. Lisa twitched the reins ever so slightly. Chocolate's ears perked up. She seemed alert. She was waiting for another signal.

"See, it works!" Kate said. "You've got her attention."

Lisa now put all of her own attention to the job in front of her.

"Go!" Christine called out, clicking the stopwatch.

Lisa did just as she'd seen Jeannie do. She kicked Chocolate and used the end of her reins as a whip. Chocolate burst into a gallop. Lisa turned to the right and headed for the first cactus. Chocolate circled it smoothly and headed for the second. At the last second, Lisa remembered that they had to go around this one to the left. Chocolate followed her instructions, passed around it, and aimed for the final cactus. This time, Lisa remembered to keep the cactus to her left. They were so close to the bristles that she almost got scratched, but she didn't and neither did Chocolate. The two of them sprinted for the finish line.

"Yahoo!" Carole, Stevie, and Kate cheered as Lisa

approached. Christine stared at the stopwatch. Lisa just knew her time was going to be excellent, better even than any of her friends'.

She wanted to end her ride with some style. She pulled on Chocolate's reins, hoping she would perform the wonderful straight-legged stop that Jeannie and Stevie had done. It worked, in a way. Chocolate got her signal and came to an instant halt. Unfortunately, Lisa wasn't quite prepared for it. She kept going, right up and over Chocolate's shoulder and onto the hard ground.

"Great finale!" Stevie teased, giving her a hand.

Lisa was a little annoyed at herself and was about to take it out on Stevie, but Christine stopped her.

"Twenty-nine seconds," Christine said.

"But I ended up in the dirt!"

"I just checked the rule book," Christine said, pocketing the stopwatch so she could give Lisa a congratulatory hug. "It doesn't say anything about having to stay on your horse after the race. Of course, the judges might prefer the more traditional dismount . . ."

"That was great!" Carole said. "You were really terrific. Can you give me some pointers on technique?"

Suddenly, Lisa felt as is she were standing on top of the world. Carole Hanson wanted help from *her*?

"Of course I can," Lisa said graciously. "And you can help me, too."

"Sure," Carole agreed. "What do you want to know?"

"How do I stop?"

On that note, the girls were ready to do some serious practicing.

"HOW DO YOU think they're doing with the busted pipes in Willow Creek?" Stevie asked her friends. The camp-out was over, the campsite was cleaned up, and the five girls were on their horses, heading back to The Bar None.

"Beats me," Carole said. "Why? You think we're doing so badly on our practice that you want to skip the rodeo and go home?"

"That's one thought," Stevie said. "What I was actually hoping, though, was that the pipes wouldn't be fixed for weeks so we'd have to stay here."

"No way," Kate said. "Once we have our triumphant

success at the rodeo, The Bar None will be filled with paying guests. We won't have room anymore for moochers!"

Lisa only half listened to the teasing. She and Christine were at the end of the group. Christine seemed unusually quiet.

"What's up?" Lisa asked.

"I was just thinking about our costumes," Christine said.

"I've been worrying about that, too," Lisa agreed. "I mean, when I think of cowboys and costumes, I start thinking about fancy stitched shirts, with piping and rhinestones, and tooled leather boots and silver-studded bridles. We don't have the time to do all that."

"To say nothing of the money!" Christine added. "And when I think of dressing up, all I can picture is what the tourists imagine is traditional American Indian garb—you know, feathered headdresses and stuff like that. We certainly don't have the time to do that, either."

"To say nothing of the wampum!" Lisa remarked.

Christine laughed. "That's right."

"So that leaves us with two goals—fast and cheap. *That* makes me think of T-shirts."

"You know, we could write something on them . . ."

"We could even get them in a bright color so they stand out . . ."

". . . front *and* back."

". . . maybe red?"

"I think we're onto something!"

"You bet we are."

"My mom's an artist. She's got all the paints and everything we could need."

"I've got the funniest feeling that this is going to be cool," Lisa said. "Really cool."

"So why don't we all meet at my house tonight after dinner to make our parade outfits?"

By the time Christine left them to head for her own house, the plan was made. Christine would have the art supplies. The others would buy and bring the T-shirts.

ELI WAS WORKING hard in the corral, practicing for the rodeo, when they arrived. The Saddle Club untacked their horses and let them out into the pasture with the rest of the herd. It only took a few minutes for them to stow their sleeping bags in the bunkhouse, tell Phyllis and Frank that they were back safely, and return to the corral to watch Eli.

The corral was set up for steer wrestling. Eli and a cowboy the girls didn't recognize were on horseback. Between them, Jeannie seemed to be in charge of the steer. The steer was confined to a little pen and was fussing to get out of it.

"Go!" Eli yelled. Jeannie released the steer and reached to give him a slap on his flank. It was unnecessary. He'd already burst out of the pen before she could touch him.

The other cowboy started chasing after the steer, and Eli came immediately after him.

The girls knew now that the hazer's job was to keep the steer running straight so that Eli could reach him. The cowboy didn't seem to know it, though. The steer took a turn to the right, in front of the hazer, away from Eli, and just kept on going. It wasn't going to matter how fast Eli could ride or how well he could wrestle the steer: If he couldn't reach the animal, he couldn't win the event. Eli drew his horse to a halt and scowled at the hazer.

"Gee, I'm sorry, Eli," the hazer said. "Guess we'll just have to try it again. I sure hope the steer at the rodeo behaves better than this one."

Carole leaned over to her friends. "Doesn't look to me like the steer is the problem here."

"You think so?" Lisa asked in surprise. "I know he's supposed to keep the steer straight, but it looked like the steer just ran wild. He couldn't help that, could he?"

"He's supposed to help it. That's his job," Stevie said.

"Come on, Derek, round up the steer and let's try again," Eli said.

Derek removed his rope from the pommel of the saddle, swung it easily in the air, and lofted it to where the still-running steer was going to be when it landed. The steer ran right into the noose. Derek yanked at the lariat to tighten the noose and brought the animal to a halt.

"Nice roping!" Kate said. "I wouldn't have thought he could do that. . . ."

"Strange," Christine said. "I wouldn't have thought so, either."

"What are you talking about?" Lisa asked.

"I think I understand what they mean. Watch closely," Carole told her.

Eli and Derek tried it again. This time, Derek kept close to the steer and kept him to the left, so far left that Derek and the steer had crossed in front of Eli before Eli could even catch up to them.

Derek seemed about to start a new round of apologies, but Eli cut him off.

"I don't know about you, but I'm getting tired. Why don't we call it a day and start again tomorrow afternoon. How about two-thirty?"

"Sure thing, Eli," Derek said. "Sure thing." Derek dismounted to lead his horse to the trough for a drink of water. It was only when he was walking on the ground that Stevie noticed he was wearing the same kind of duster that the wranglers had worn at The Dapper Dude. She liked the way it looked. It was old-fashioned and practical, designed to protect the rider. At the same time, it was very stylish.

"That's really kind of cool, isn't it?" she said to her friends.

"Think we should wear dusters instead of T-shirts?" Lisa asked.

"No, not really. We probably shouldn't take a chance on anything getting in our way when we race. But they are cool," Stevie said.

"Definitely," Carole agreed.

Once Derek's horse had had his fill, Derek re-
mounted and rode off the ranch. He tipped his hat
ever so slightly as he passed the girls. Stevie thought
that was cool, too.

"I'M FINISHED WITH my front!" Stevie announced,
holding up her red T-shirt for everybody to admire. It
read,

FINEST DUDES AROUND

"And I'm done with my back," Lisa said, holding
hers next to Stevie's. It was simple. It just said,

O

That was the branding symbol that meant Bar None,
so that the full message of their shirts was that they
were the finest dudes around, bar none. That seemed
to all of them to be an appropriate message.

"You think Jeannie would wear one of these?" Carole asked. "I mean, the more people who are wearing
them, the more people will become familiar with the
ranch. It's kind of like a walking advertisement, isn't
it?"

The girls agreed that that was a great idea. Phyllis
Devine had bought some extra shirts, so they pro-
ceeded to put their design on them.

"I'm done first, so I'll do Jeannie's," Stevie offered.
She selected one that looked as if it would fit, ironed it
so it was completely wrinkle-free, and began to paint it
carefully. Stevie was good at art. It was one of the few

things, aside from horseback riding, that she had any patience for. She chatted as she worked. "You know, talking about Jeannie makes me think about Eli. And thinking about Eli makes me think about Derek. He's cute, isn't he?"

"Cute, maybe," Carole said, "but *good,* no way. He could cost Eli the event."

Lisa looked up from her shirt. Her friends had reminded her of something she wanted to ask them. "You know, I didn't get what you guys were talking about today when he was roping the steer. What was wrong?"

"Well, he was so *good* at it," Kate said.

"So?" Lisa knew she was missing something, but she didn't know what. Kate explained it to her.

"Roping that well is hard, really hard. It takes a lot of practice. Hazing is a little tricky, but it's not very difficult. So the question is, why is somebody so good at the hard part and so bad at the easy part?"

"I see," Lisa said.

"But the *real* question," Stevie pointed out, "is, why did Eli go all the way to town and find a stranger to do his hazing when he's got an adoring and able fan named Jeannie Sanders right here who is an expert rider, as we saw yesterday, and who could do it for him perfectly well?"

There were a few seconds of silence as the other girls looked at each other.

"That certainly is a real question," Christine said at last.

"It hadn't occurred to me, but you're absolutely right," Kate said.

"I'll bet you anything it's occurred to Jeannie," Stevie said.

"So, why didn't she offer?" Carole asked.

"Maybe there's some kind of rule," Lisa suggested. "You read all that stuff, Christine. Did you see anything?"

"I remember that only men are allowed to compete in most events except barrel racing, and that's girls all under eighteen. But a hazer isn't a competitor. There shouldn't be any reason why Jeannie couldn't do it."

"Except there is a reason—one reason—and his name is Eli. When it comes to Jeannie, the man is blind, totally blind. Now, if only there were a way to open his eyes . . ."

"Hold it, Cupid," Carole said, interrupting Stevie. "This is none of our business."

Stevie thought about what Carole said. She really liked both Jeannie and Eli, and she hated the fact that Jeannie was so crazy about him while he didn't notice her at all. Carole was right, though. That wasn't their business. But there was something else to consider.

"Some of it isn't our business, but the part about Eli's hazer *is* our business," Stevie argued. "After all, we've made it our business to make The Bar None look good at the rodeo. Derek could ruin it for both Eli and The Bar None. Jeannie would do a much better job, so we should see to it that she does it."

"Swell idea, but how?" Kate asked.

The question hung in the air, unanswered. Eli had the right to choose his own hazer, and he'd chosen Derek. Stevie shook her head. She didn't have an answer. Resignedly, she picked up the brush and continued working on Jeannie's shirt. That was something she *could* do something about.

IT WAS TIME. Lisa couldn't believe it. It was finally
Saturday morning. She didn't think she'd ever been
busier than she'd been for the past few days, practicing, polishing, talking, planning, hoping. Now it was
time. All the work was behind them. The parade was
about to start. The rodeo was about to begin. And in
just a few hours The Bar None Riders would find out
whether all that practice had done them any good.

But first, the fun.

"Everybody sit up straight. Smile! Give those people
out there a show!"

Lisa reached down and brushed a small smudge of

dirt off her boot. She smoothed her Bar None T-shirt and adjusted her hat. She sat up straight. She was *ready*.

The Bar None Riders were all together in a row in the parade. In fact, their team had been selected to lead the barrel-racing section. Kate even got to hold a banner. Lisa glanced at it. She knew that it was just chance that their team's name had been selected to lead, but it still made her feel special, and she wanted to look that way. She wanted to give the people a show!

The parade was more of a grand march than a parade. All of the contestants were in it, dressed in their fanciest, best cowboy clothes. Their horses were as shiny clean as any horse-show horses The Saddle Club had ever seen. The whole place was afire with bright colors, gleaming leather, and lively horses. It was wonderful!

"Barrel racers, go!" the Master of Ceremonies yelled out.

Kate touched her spurs to Spot's belly and the horse spurted through the gate into the arena. Carole, Stevie, and Christine followed, and Lisa brought up the rear. Behind her, three more barrel-racing teams pranced into the arena. The last was the team from The Dapper Dude. Lisa had noticed them in their stylish cowgirl outfits when they'd arrived. Then she'd decided that the less she thought about them, the better she'd feel. It wasn't easy to not think about them. It wasn't easy to feel good, either, until she entered the arena.

As soon as she was in, she forgot everything but the parade and the crowd and the rodeo. It was magical!

The parade was planned to snake all around the arena in a complex design, marked out by rodeo judges. The line of horses crossed itself several times, meaning that the riders had to take turns going through the crossing point. It was the sort of exercise Stevie, Lisa, and Carole had done a lot of when they'd worked on their drill-team routine. They were pretty good at it and not one of them made a mistake in the parade. The crowd cheered. The riders waved. Lisa spotted Kate's and Christine's parents in the stands. The Bar None Riders waved at them especially hard.

The parade organizer had designed the route so that they all rode around the arena single file and then exited, circling outside the arena, and then reentered in ranks of four for the finale and the singing of the national anthem. The first section of the parade was done at a lope, the final entry was at a trot. And all of this was done without any practice at all!

It seemed that the parade was over in no time. Before she knew it, Lisa was sitting in the saddle with her hand over her heart, singing with the crowd and gazing at the American flag. When the last note died out, the parade moved out of the arena and the rodeo began.

*　　*　　*

THERE WERE SIX main events in the Two Mile Creek Rodeo. First, there were the men's events: saddle-bronc riding, bareback riding, calf roping, and steer wrestling; then came the girls' barrel racing, and finally, bull riding. There was a lunch break between calf roping and steer wrestling, and during the lunch break, there would be demonstrations of nontraditional rodeo events—wild-cow milking, buffalo riding, and clowning.

"I can't believe how much is going on today!" Christine said, checking the timetable in the program. "And we've got to corral our horses right away so we can be back in time for Eli's first event."

Carole smiled to herself. Ever since they'd registered for the barrel-racing event and the woman had handed them the schedule, Christine had been like a mother hen. It wasn't so bad, though. After all, somebody had to know everything that was going on and get them to places on time. It seemed that the woman had known what she was doing when she'd given the materials to Christine. Carole hated to think what would have happened if she'd given them to Stevie!

The girls put their horses in their assigned corral, stowed their tack, and went to find Eli so they could cheer him on.

". . . and he's out!" the P.A. blasted. The first saddle-bronc rider was on his way.

The girls ran over to the fence to watch. The horse sprang out of the gate, bucked and twisted sideways, and the cowboy flew over his head and into the dirt.

"Eli can do better than that," Kate said. The other girls agreed.

The next cowboy did better. He stayed on his bronc for the full ten seconds, but the horse wasn't giving him much trouble, either.

"According to this," Christine explained, once again consulting the booklet they'd gotten from the registration lady, "the cowboy and the horse are both judged equally, so the cowboy who is on a wild horse can get a lot more points than a rider on an easy horse. All the riders want the toughest horses. That's true in saddle-bronc and bareback riding."

"Bull riding, too?" Stevie asked.

"I don't think so," Kate said. "From what I've heard, all the bulls are hard to ride. They are *mean.*"

"I'm glad Eli's not in that one, then. I wouldn't want him to get hurt," Lisa said.

Just then the girls spotted Eli. There were only a few riders left ahead of him. They walked over to cheer him on. He was talking with another cowboy, while Jeannie stood at his elbow.

"I rode Jester two weeks ago at a county rodeo," the other cowboy was saying. "He's a good one. Bucks straight, true, and hard. You can score on him. Watch out, though. He'll yank at the rope, so you got to let him have some length or you'll end up eating dirt."

"Thanks," Eli said, and Carole could tell he really meant it.

"Don't mention it," the cowboy said. "You'll do the same for me."

"That's nice of him," Kate said to Eli when the other cowboy left.

"Everybody around here seems like that," Eli told her. "Everybody's got advice for everybody else and most of it seems to be good."

"Four eighty-three—you're up next!" a starter said, calling to Eli.

Jeannie yanked at his arm. Carole noticed that she was being a bit of a mother hen herself. As usual, though, Eli didn't seem to notice one way or the other.

"Push your hat back a bit," she said.

"Then it won't stay on my head," he protested.

"That's the idea, see. If your hat flies off, it makes it look as if you're riding out the tough bucks, no matter what's happening."

Eli grinned. "Clever!" he said, pushing the brim of his hat up, just a bit.

The girls all climbed on the fence of the saddling area where Jester was being prepared for Eli. Faster than they'd ever seen a horse tacked, the wranglers cinched the saddle and put on the halter with the lead rope that Eli would hold.

A tired, bruised cowboy limped back to the edge of the arena. The P.A. announcer told the crowd that Eli Grimes was next. In a matter of seconds, Eli lowered himself onto Jester's back, slid his boots into the stirrups, took hold of the rope that served as a rein, measured a length that would allow Jester to yank, but would give him some control, and went out.

"Spur him! Spur him!" Jeannie yelled, as if Eli needed the reminder.

Jester bucked into action. He pulled forward, yanking at the rope, and flung his rear legs up into the air, tossing Eli forward. Eli's hat flew off. The crowd went "Ooooooh!" The girls clapped wildly. Jeannie just grinned.

Eli swung his legs forward and back with the bucking movement of the horse. It was just what he was supposed to do. Jester bucked high and hard, but he bucked regularly, rhythmically. Every time the horse rose, Eli rose with him, landing hard, but balanced, staying in the saddle, more or less, feet in the stirrups, free hand held high and waving for balance.

At last, the buzzer sounded. One of the pick-up men helped Eli off the bronc and onto the back of his horse while the other released the bronc's flank cinch. Jester calmed down immediately and returned to the corral. The crowd clapped wildly, especially when Eli picked up his hat and put it back on his head. He walked proudly back to the fence where his biggest fans were waiting, and tipped his dusty hat to the crowd while they applauded his score.

"Nice job!" Jeannie said proudly, basking in the glory of the moment with Eli.

"Thanks," he said. "And thanks for the tip about my hat. I think the crowd liked it."

"The crowd *loved* it," Carole declared.

When Eli's score flashed on the board, it was clear

that the judges loved it, too. Eli and Jester had both scored well, and Eli was now in first place. There were only four more riders in the event.

"At least I'll place," Eli said. "I've got to place in all my events. It'll mean money for the ranch, but mostly it'll give me a shot at that scholarship."

"You won't just place, you'll win," Stevie said.

"Not likely," Eli told her. "See, the best riders and horses seem to be coming up behind me in this event. Unfortunately I've just given them a score to shoot for. I'll do okay here. My best event is calf roping. The one I've got to worry about is steer wrestling."

"Me, too," Stevie said.

Carole looked at her. It was a funny thing for Stevie to have said. It was an odd way to put it, but she knew exactly what Stevie meant. They were all worried about the steer wrestling.

The Bar None group found a place to stand by the edge of the arena to watch the final riders in the saddle-bronc contest. They were really good.

"This one's been doing this for years," Eli said. "He's a shoo-in for first place."

Carole watched closely. Eli was right. In ten seconds, the cowboy showed the crowd and the judges just how good good really could be.

"He outspurred me, outstyled me, and outrode me," Eli said. "And, his horse was tougher."

"But his hat stayed on!" Jeannie observed.

It turned out that the judges agreed with Eli. The

experienced cowboy outscored Eli, but he was the only one who did.

"You got second!" Stevie said, giving him a congratulatory hug.

"And I'm satisfied with that," Eli said. The girls decided they would be satisfied, too.

"Look, I've got to ready my ropes for my next event. Why don't you all wander around and check out the rest of the rodeo, watch the bareback riding—whatever."

"You tired of your adoring fans?" Stevie teased.

"Naw," Eli said. "Never get tired of that. I've just got to work now. See you all later, okay?"

Apparently Jeannie didn't think that "all" applied to her. She followed Eli to the corral, leaving the girls to themselves.

"Want to check out the souvenirs?" Christine asked. "My mother is selling some of her pottery today."

Since there was a break between events, the girls decided it would be a good time to check out all the booths. Carole had noticed on the way in that there was a large selection of western gear, everything from turquoise jewelry and boots to saddles and kerchiefs. She wanted to examine some of the things. And besides, she wanted to see Mrs. Lonetree's pottery selection. She did such beautiful work. Carole hoped she'd find something her father might like.

However, before they even got to Mrs. Lonetree's booth, they saw something even more interesting than

Indian pottery, cowboy belt buckles, or bright red ker-chiefs. They saw Derek.

"Shhh!" Stevie said, holding her arm out to stop her friends. They all saw Derek at the same instant and they flattened themselves against a wall where he couldn't see them, but they could hear him. The reason they did that was that he was talking to someone, and that someone was none other than Rule-Book Marshall from The Dapper Dude.

"You ready for this afternoon?" Marshall asked.

"Easy as pie," Derek said.

"Doing it's easy, making it look good isn't," Marshall cautioned.

"Don't you worry," Derek said. "That guy's never going to get within ten feet of his steer. I've got a hundred ways to make it go bad. He's only seen ninety-nine of them so far!"

"I'll take care of you later," Marshall said. "After I win the event."

The two shook hands and parted. Fortunately, neither of them walked past where the astonished girls were standing. Neither of them saw five girls getting angry, and neither saw five girls determined to get even.

"WE'VE GOT TO tell Eli!" Carole said as soon as Derek and Marshall were out of earshot.

"No way!" Stevie said. "It would just upset him, and he doesn't need that right now."

"But we can't let Derek ruin the event for him!" Kate said, her voice rising with concern.

"And he won't, either!" Stevie told her friends. "What we have to do instead is to fix the situation so that Eli never knows what went right. Later, like tonight, we can tell him everything. Maybe. But not now."

"So?" Lisa asked expectantly.

"I don't know yet," Stevie said. She seemed a little annoyed. Carole suspected she was actually annoyed with herself. "It's only been about fifteen seconds since we learned what the problem was. I don't have a solution yet, okay?"

"Okay, okay," Christine said, trying to calm Stevie down. "Take as long as you want. As long as you come up with something!"

"I always have, haven't I?" Stevie asked.

Carole slung her arm across Stevie's shoulder. "One of the things The Saddle Club has been able to rely on is that when some crazy scheme is called for, Stevie will be the one to come up with it."

"Yeah, and one thing I've been able to rely on is that when one of my crazy schemes needs some crazy people to carry it out, The Saddle Club has always come through," Stevie said. "That's what friends are for, right?" They all agreed. "So, let's go watch the bareback riding and see Eli take first prize in the calf roping. That's sure to clear my head enough to figure out how to solve this problem, which actually seems more like two, no, three problems."

"*Three?*" Christine said, surprised.

Stevie nodded and counted them off on her fingers. "One is getting rid of Derek. Two is getting Eli a hazer he can trust. And three is getting him to notice Jeannie and preferably fall in love with her."

"And four is solving all of these problems without Eli being aware that we're doing it," Carole reminded her.

"Hmmmmm." Stevie looked thoughtful.

Carole knew that meant the wheels were turning. It was a good time to leave Stevie to let her figure it out herself.

"Come on," Carole said. "I think Phyllis and Frank have saved us some seats. Let's go watch the next event."

Bareback riding, it turned out, was quite a bit like saddle-bronc riding except there was no saddle and no rein at all. There was just a rig around the horse's belly called a surcingle that provided a handle at about the same place the pommel would have been on a saddled horse.

It was wild riding all right. More than one cowboy ended up in the dirt. One man was thrown so badly that he had to hobble off to the ambulance that was parked by the main corral.

"Thank goodness that didn't happen to Eli," Phyllis remarked.

"I'll say. He'd be useless as a wrangler with a couple of broken ribs!" Frank chuckled.

"Daddy!" Kate cried.

"I'm joking. I'm just joking!" Frank said quickly.

"I don't think the girls found it funny, Frank," Phyllis told him.

"I got that message, too. However, there's another message here and it's that rodeo riding is a dangerous sport."

"Don't worry, Frank," Carole said. "That one came through to us loud and clear."

They were quiet then as they enjoyed the remainder of the bareback riding. When the last competitor was finished and the final standings were announced, Stevie made an announcement as well.

"I've got it," she said.

"So, tell," Kate said excitedly. "What is it?"

"We don't have to do anything until the lunch break. I'll tell then. Besides, I still have to work out the details. For now, just enjoy the show. It'll be good, but the show this afternoon will be even better!" There was a grin on Stevie's face and a twinkle in her eyes that told her friends that they could, indeed, relax. Stevie had a plan and it was sure to be a great one!

Lisa leaned forward to get the best possible view of the calf roping. After all, this was Eli's strongest event. She didn't want to miss anything.

She couldn't believe how good some of the cowboys were, and she couldn't believe how intricate all the equipment was. At first, all she saw was the cowboy's swinging lariat. With the help of an experienced fan sitting next to her, she began to see that the event had a lot more to it than that. The cowboys actually had three ropes. One was the lariat. Another was the small rope he used to tie up any three of the calf's legs once the animal was down. The third rope was a complicated rig that went from the cowboy's waist around the pommel of the saddle and through the horse's bridle. As the cowboy ran forward to the calf, this rope tightened, putting pressure on the bit. That, in turn, signaled the horse to back up, making the rope from the saddle to the calf taut, and keeping the calf on the ground so the cowboy could tie his legs.

"Wow!" Lisa said when she finally understood what all the rigging was about. "That's something!" She shared her new knowledge with her friends. "Boy, if the whole thing is off by just a few inches, it doesn't work at all."

"This event is really a partnership between the cowboy and his horse," Carole observed.

"And that's why Eli's so good at it," Kate said. "Nobody in the world is better with horses than Eli. It's like he can really talk to them."

"A lot of cowboys talk to their horses," Christine remarked wryly. "It gets lonely out there on the roundup trail!"

"Talking is one thing. Making them understand is another," Kate said. "Eli is just plain good."

"And Eli is just plain up next," Lisa said, quieting her friends.

The buzzer sounded. A calf dashed out of the chute and Eli was right behind it. Almost as soon as Lisa could see Eli, she could see his rope lofting in the air toward the calf. The calf seemed to run right into the loop. Then, like clockwork, Eli was on the ground, running toward the calf, while his horse was backing away from him, tightening the calf's rope and keeping the animal on the ground.

Eli leaned over the calf, grabbed one of its legs, looped the short rope around the ankle, grabbed two other legs, circled them with the end of the rope, looped it into a knot, and raised his hands in triumph.

"Wowee!" the announcer yelled, obviously impressed. "I think we've got a winning time here, folks. Mr. Eli Grimes of The Bar None has just broken the record for the Two Mile Creek Rodeo. His new record is eight point seven-eight seconds! Let's give this man a hand!"

And they did. In fact, everybody in the entire arena rose to their feet and gave him a standing ovation. It was wonderful. And not only was that good for Eli, but it was also good for The Bar None. Lisa saw Kate give her father a squeeze. It was really something to be happy about.

The rest of the calf roping was almost a letdown after Eli's performance. The riders knew it and the crowd knew it. There were some good times, there were some flashy performances, but it was clear that there was only one Eli. And one of the nicest things was that every time the announcer said Eli's name, he also mentioned The Bar None.

It almost surprised Lisa when lunch break was announced. She'd been feeling so good about Eli's performance that she'd forgotten about Stevie's secret scheme. She'd also forgotten that their own performance was coming up. It was one thing to be excited about Eli. It was another thing altogether to think about their barrel race. What if they blew it? She shook her head. *Think positive*, she told herself. It wasn't easy.

"Come on," Stevie said. "We've got to practice."

If somebody else had said that, Lisa might have wondered what it was she wanted to practice, but with Stevie, it was easy. It was time to practice treachery!

"OKAY, GIRLS," STEVIE said when they'd reached the corral with the practice barrel-race course. "You all wait over here. Saddle up the horses if you want. Do anything to make it look good. Eli's going to be here in a few minutes. He's coming to give us some last-minute pointers. Make sure you've got some questions to ask him, okay?"

"No problem," Carole said. "But what will you be doing?"

"I'll be setting the trap," Stevie said mysteriously. She loved her plan, and she was sure it would work, but she didn't want to reveal the whole thing until it was a success. Since there were so many problems to solve at once, there were a lot of pieces to move around. Sometimes, she knew, her friends did a better job if they didn't know just what she was up to.

Stevie left the group waiting at the barrel-racing corral and began Phase One of her plan. She went in search of her first quarry: Eli.

She found him being congratulated by his fellow calf ropers near the registration tent. Jeannie was there, too—as she'd expected.

"Oh, I'm so glad I found you!" Stevie told both of them. They didn't know how much she meant it!

"What's up, Stevie?" Eli asked.

"It's the team," she said, letting a bit of panic creep into her voice. "They're getting the worst stage fright. They're all over by the practice course and they're scared and worried. Can you go over and talk to them? Both of you?"

"Oh, sure," Eli said.

"Thanks. I'll be there in a minute. I've got to find the ladies' room first."

"I'll show you where it is," Jeannie offered. Stevie didn't want that at all.

"Oh, no," she said hurriedly. "The team needs both of you. Right away!" She hoped she sounded urgent. The last thing she wanted was to have Jeannie along with her. "I can find the ladies' room by myself. Go with Eli, okay?"

Fortunately, going places with Eli was an activity Jeannie didn't need to be forced into. Obediently, she followed him to the barrel-racing corral.

As soon as they were out of sight, Stevie began Phase Two of her plan. She had to find Derek.

She spied him on the other side of the arena, still hanging around the souvenir stands. Probably waiting to see if there were any messages from Marshall, Stevie thought. She had suspected as much and was glad for it since it meant he'd been lying low—and hadn't seen Eli for a long time.

Stevie nodded hello when he spotted her. "Too bad about Eli," she said as she approached him.

"What do you mean, 'too bad'?" Derek asked suspiciously. "He took first place, didn't he?"

"Sure, but then who knew that horse would go wild on him?"

"What horse?" Derek asked.

"Oh, you didn't hear?" Stevie hoped she sounded very surprised. Derek shook his head, bewildered. "But you're going to be so disappointed. He's out for the day. He was helping one of the wranglers round up the broncs, slipped on some mud, and a bronc took after him. He got badly bruised and cut. They took him off in the ambulance. They think he's got a concussion. We're going to meet him in the hospital right after the barrel racing."

"Oh," Derek said. He sounded surprised, but not too disappointed. He adjusted his voice and tried again. "Oh, that's terrible," he said, sounding much more sincere this time.

"I bet you want to get right over to the hospital now and be with him, don't you?"

Derek just stared at her for a second. Then he came to his senses, as Stevie had known he would. Of course he couldn't let Stevie know he had no intention of going to the hospital. With Eli out of commission, Derek's job was done. The only thing for him to do was to leave the rodeo, but the last place he would go was the hospital, which was about fifty miles away. Sure as anything, he'd be back at The Dapper Dude within a few minutes.

"We'll see you at the hospital later, then?" Stevie asked.

"Sure thing," Derek promised.

Stevie knew a lie when she heard one. It made her feel good that her plan was working so well. She made Derek promise to tell Eli how much they all cared and that they were rooting for him, and they were dedicating their barrel race to him. She was afraid she might have gone too far with that one, but Derek seemed to swallow it and promised to tell Eli.

Derek couldn't wait to get to his pickup truck. Soon Stevie found herself waving good-bye to him through a cloud of dust. She was glad for the dust. There was no way Derek could see her triumphant grin through it!

"Phase Three," she said out loud. She returned to the barrel-racing area and found the stage set. Jeannie was answering questions. Eli assured the team that she knew what she was talking about.

"The thing you want to do is to lean into the turn," Jeannie was saying. "But not too much or you'll lose your balance."

"Listen to her, girls," Eli said. "She knows what she's talking about."

"Before you come out of a turn, you should already be signaling the horse for the straightaway gallop. Don't let him ease up just because he's done something right."

"But—" Christine began.

"No buts," Eli said firmly. "There's no better precision rider in the county than Jeannie. Do what she says."

Stevie couldn't believe her ears. It was a perfect cue for her.

"Say, Eli," she interrupted. He looked up at her. "Something funny just happened."

"What, you signed up for another contest and you want me to tell you what it is?" Eli loved to tease Stevie.

"That's very funny, but no, this is *serious* funny."

"What's the matter?" he asked.

"Well, I was on my way back here and I saw that guy who's supposed to be hazing for you. What's his name—Derek?"

"I've been looking all over for him," Eli said. "It's time for us to go over some things."

"Well, you're not going to find him," Stevie said. "He's gone."

"Gone?"

"Yeah. He saw me, told me to tell you something came up and he couldn't stick around, and that he was really sorry, but before I could ask him what the problem was, he was in his truck and hightailing it out of here."

"Gone?" Eli repeated, stunned. Stevie saw her teammates exchange sly glances. She knew they'd suspect her fine hand. She had to tie up the loose ends quickly before a giggle gave her away.

"But where in blazes am I going to find a hazer just fifteen minutes before the steer-wrestling event begins?"

Stevie let the question hang in the air for a few seconds. She scratched her head thoughtfully. She was going to rub her chin, but she thought that might be a bit too much. "How about the best precision rider in the county?" she asked.

"Great idea," Eli said, "but who is he?"

"It's a she. And you're standing next to her," Carole said, reminding him of his own words a few minutes earlier.

"*Jeannie?*" he asked.

"I do," she said.

MOST OF THE barrel racers spent the time during the steer-wrestling event checking their horses and their tack and readying themselves for their race. But The Bar None Riders were in the stands. They weren't going to miss a minute of the steer wrestling. They'd have to rush before their own event, but that didn't matter compared to watching Eli and Jeannie's performance.

"This is either the longest or shortest event there is," Stevie remarked after watching one cowboy down a steer in less than six seconds and another chase the frightened animal all over the ring. That poor man never caught up with the steer.

"All these other guys can take as long as they want," Kate said. "It's Eli who will be done with it the fastest."

"Eli and *Jeannie,*" Stevie said, reminding her of the good deed The Saddle Club had done.

"Keep your fingers crossed," Christine said. "The last time I saw them, Eli was still staring at her like he'd just discovered she was alive."

"Love does funny things to people," Lisa remarked. "At least that's what I've noticed."

"Hmmmmm," was all Stevie would say.

By the time it was Eli's turn, most of the contestants had already gone and the competition was very stiff. Eli didn't expect to win. All he really hoped was to do respectably against the clock. When he was applying for his rodeo scholarship, his total score was what mattered, whether he placed or not.

"Our next competitor is Eli Grimes and we've got an unusual story here, ladies and gentlemen," the announcer said. "We've got this rodeo's first woman hazer, Ms. Jeannie Sanders. This pair works together on The Bar None ranch. Let's see how they work together at the Two Mile Creek Rodeo!"

The crowd clapped enthusiastically. They remembered Eli's performance in the calf-roping event. The Saddle Club exchanged triumphant grins. This was all good for Eli, but it was *great* for the ranch.

The steer was rounded into the chute and the

starter, who would shoot him out, climbed in behind. Eli and Jeannie took their places.

The chute's gate opened with a *clack!* and the steer shot out into the ring. Stevie saw the whole thing as if it were in slow motion. Jeannie's horse sprang after the steer, keeping him on a straight path. Eli's horse burst out of his starting gate, neared Jeannie and the steer in a split second, and began the hard work. When the head of Eli's horse was even with the rump of the steer, Eli slid to his right, lowering himself onto the steer. His right arm came up under the steer's right horn from behind. His left arm circled from in front. Then Eli was off his horse and moving forward with the momentum of the running steer. His own heels dug into the dirt. He used all his weight to pull the steer toward him. Then, just as the steer's flanks rose to protest, Eli twisted, turning the steer's neck toward the ground. The rest of the animal followed. And it was over!

Eli stood up, releasing the steer, and then turned to look at the clock. Four point nine-three seconds. He was in first place!

Jeannie couldn't help herself. She rode over to where Eli stood, bringing him his horse, but when she reached him, she slid down off her own saddle and flung her arms around him. He was so happy, he hugged her back. Then, to the surprise and delight of everybody in the arena, Jeannie kissed him. And to the surprise and delight of everybody, especially The Bar None Riders, Eli kissed her back!

"Whew!" Stevie said. But nobody heard her. Everybody was standing up, yelling and clapping.

"He's got it. Let's go," Kate said. She was right. Even if another cowboy rode faster and Eli came in second, they had still won. He'd beat his own best time, and everybody in the crowd knew that he rode for The Bar None. That kiss in the center of the arena had left an indelible impression on everybody! The girls left the bleachers and headed back to get their horses ready for the barrel racing.

"You know," Kate said as they walked. "It doesn't really matter now if we win. Eli's done all the work for us."

"Eli and Jeannie," Stevie corrected her.

"Eli and Jeannie and *Stevie*," Carole said.

"Oh, it's teamwork. It's all teamwork," Stevie said modestly.

"One of the secrets of successful teamwork is letting the team members do the things they are best at," Lisa said. "And on our team, there is nobody better at telling whoppers and carrying out crazy schemes than Stevie."

They all agreed with that and clapped Stevie on the back to congratulate her.

A FEW MINUTES later, the team was all business again. It was time to compete in the barrel racing. The girls checked their horses' tack and then put their red team T-shirts back on. Each girl also put on a new white cowboy hat. They did look like a team, but, Lisa thought, more importantly, they felt like a team.

"Now, if only we can *perform* like a team," she muttered to herself, recalling the several times she'd ended in the dirt.

The way the team barrel-racing competition worked at Two Mile Creek Rodeo was that the number one riders from each team would race in turn, then the number two riders, and so on. When all five riders from all four teams had gone, the worst score from each team would be dropped out. The final score was the total of the four best scores on each team.

The Bar None Riders had chosen their order with care. Carole would begin, then Lisa, Stevie, Christine, and finally Kate. They wanted to get a good edge with a strong first rider and they wanted to end with the best. Lisa, Stevie, and Christine were just to do the best they could.

Lisa knew she was the least-experienced rider on the team and her score would probably be the one dropped out. She was determined to have fun anyway.

The girls didn't know anything about the first two teams, and they didn't really care. It was the fourth team, the one that followed them, that they knew they had to beat. That was the team from The Dapper Dude. The girls from The Dapper Dude were dressed for the occasion, too. Each of them was wearing a sparkling-clean white cowgirl outfit, with fancy black piping and shiny black buttons. Lisa glanced down at her red T-shirt. It looked almost shabby compared to The Dapper Dude outfits.

Stevie yanked at her elbow. "It doesn't matter what we wear," she said firmly. "It matters how we ride."

"I know," Lisa said, but she couldn't help sounding wistful. "Sort of."

The number one riders from the first two teams told Lisa and the other riders that their biggest competition was going to be from The Dapper Dude. The announcer called their names, and the girls made it through the course all right, but even Lisa knew that they weren't fast enough to win.

"Bar None Rider Number One!" the announcer said. "Miss Carole Hanson!"

Lisa thought she heard a "Yahooo!" from the stands. It had to be Eli. She grinned.

Carole had a stiff, serious look of concentration on her face. Lisa thought she probably hadn't heard anything after her own name.

"Go!" the starter yelled.

Carole was out of the gate. She swung her horse, Berry, over to the right. He rounded the first barrel okay, though his feet seemed to slip a little and his balance was off. By the time he got to the second barrel, though, Carole was in trouble. She was going fast all right, but she was in such a hurry and Berry was so eager to please her that there was no way they'd make it!

"Slow down!" Lisa yelled, but it was too late.

Carole made Berry cut the corner too sharply. His

shoulder hit the barrel. The barrel knocked against Carole's knee, rocked perilously, and then tumbled to the ground.

"Penalty!" the announcer said. That meant that five seconds would be added to Carole's final time. There was no way that would be a winning round!

Carole completed her turn and brought Berry back to where her friends waited. Her face showed nothing, but Lisa was sure it was taking every bit of Carole's control to hide her disappointment.

"I guess it's up to you four now," Carole said, drawing into the circle her friends made for her.

Lisa didn't even notice the start of the next racer's run. Carole's words kept echoing in her head. Her penalty meant that Lisa's ride would count, no matter how bad it was. Her score couldn't be dropped out because Carole's was so high with the five-second penalty. If anybody else on the team was penalized, it would be virtually impossible for them to win. What Lisa did would matter, really matter.

It was strange and frightening to realize that she would make a difference. She hoped she'd make a difference for the better!

"Oh, that was a good one!" Stevie groaned. Lisa looked up to see a triumphant Dapper Dude rider return to her group. The score on the board indicated that The Bar None Riders really had their work cut out for them.

Now the number two riders took their turns. Once again, the riders from the other two teams didn't worry

The Bar None Riders. One team had a low score; the other had a default when the rider went the wrong way around the third barrel.

Then it was Lisa's turn.

She drew up to the starting line. The world was a blur. She was only vaguely aware of the starter. Mostly, her head was full of instructions. Lean into a turn. Don't lean too far. Go fast. Not too fast. Cut close to the barrel. Not too close. Right, left, left. Gallop. Use your spurs. Hold on. Right, left, left. Don't fall off. Don't fall off. Don't fall . . .

"Go!"

Lisa touched Chocolate with the spurs and gave her a firm whack to get her started. Chocolate flew out of the starting gate, took a sharp right, and was on her way!

Lisa had never felt anything like it. She gave the horse signals and Chocolate responded instantly, shifting to the right on the straightaway toward the second barrel, turning to the left like a pro. Chocolate got into her gallop on the way out of the turn and was at the third barrel almost before Lisa was ready. Lisa laid the reins on her neck to turn left. Chocolate turned in a flash, almost running into the barrel. Then all Lisa could see was that Chocolate's shoulder had brushed the barrel and her own foot was going to touch it, too. She squeezed her boot against the horse's side to get it out of the way, but felt it hit the barrel anyway.

There was no time to think, no time to worry. If the barrel went, it went. She leaned forward in the saddle and made Chocolate go as fast as she could. Lisa could hear the audience. "Ooooooh!" She knew it was the barrel. She waited for the dreaded word from the announcer, but it didn't come. As she crossed the finish line, the crowd applauded and her teammates bounced with delight in their saddles. Lisa brought Chocolate to a perfect straight-legged halt—this time staying in the saddle—and turned around to look. At the other end of the arena, the barrel was still rocking slightly, but it was upright!

"Good time, Lisa Atwood!" the announcer said.

Lisa couldn't help grinning. Carole reached over and squeezed one hand. "Great job. Thanks," she said.

"My pleasure," Lisa said. "Really." She squeezed back.

The second Dapper Dude rider wasn't as good as the first, but she was good. The race wasn't over yet, and everybody knew it.

Stevie did well. She didn't try to do anything too fancy. She just went fast and didn't knock anything down. Carole and Lisa welcomed her back with a hug. They'd certainly learned a lot about barrel racing in just a few days. But would it be enough?

The third girl from The Dapper Dude seemed the weakest of that group. She had trouble controlling her horse, and her time was quite slow.

"That's their drop-out score," Carole said.

"Maybe somebody else will be slower," Lisa said hopefully.

"I doubt it," Carole said. "I've been watching the

other two girls and you can tell they know what they're doing."

"This isn't good news, is it?" Lisa asked.

"Probably not," Carole said, "but at least we've got two very good scores so far. And we'll probably get two more."

Then it was Christine's turn. Christine didn't have the show experience that Kate did, but she was an excellent rider. As soon as she left the gate, Lisa knew she'd do fine. And she did. Christine's horse, Arrow, seemed to be having a lot of fun on the barrel-race course. He came out of the turns and into his straightaway gallops with a real joy in his pounding step. It was clean, it was fast, and it was good.

The team welcomed Christine back with lots of hugs. Things were looking up.

But then the next rider from The Dapper Dude got on the course. She was the best they'd ever seen. She was even better than Jeannie had been. It seemed as if she'd just left the gate when she returned. The crowd applauded for her long and loud.

The Bar None Riders were silent. They hadn't thought it possible to go through the course as fast as that girl had done it.

"I think we're looking at second place," Stevie said glumly.

"I don't mind taking second," Kate said, watching the final riders of the first two teams cover the course. "I just mind coming in behind The Dapper Dude. Now, if there's one thing I learned in all those years of competition, it's that it's not over until it's over. And so far, teammates, it's not over."

"And now the final rider from The Bar None, Miss Kate Devine!" the announcer said.

"Go for it!" Carole encouraged her.

"I will," Kate said determinedly.

A change had come over her, and Lisa couldn't help noticing it. She was no longer their friend, Kate Devine. She was Katharine Devine, championship rider—owner of thousands of ribbons, hundreds of trophies, and many memories of tough competitions. What Lisa saw in her face was serious resolve. It wasn't a vague let's-do-our-best face. It was more professional than that. It was as if Kate knew, to the millisecond, exactly how fast she would have to go to carry her team. She gazed at the course as if she were figuring out exactly where she could shave that millisecond so she could win.

"Go!" the starter cried and Kate was gone.

Lisa watched, fascinated. She'd never seen anything like it. Kate cut closer, turned faster, leaned farther than Lisa would have thought possible. Spot's shoulder brushed the top of every single barrel. Each one rocked slightly, but stayed up.

Lisa glanced at the clock while Kate raced down the final straightaway. She couldn't believe it. Kate was a full two seconds ahead of the other rider from The Dapper Dude!

"Wow, what a ride!" the announcer said. The crowd agreed. This time, too, everybody could hear Eli shouting "Yahoo!" and Jeannie was right alongside him, cheering almost as loud. Kate's parents clapped and yelled for their daughter with everybody else. The entire audience was electrified by Kate's performance.

At last the applause quieted down. It was time for the final rider from The Dapper Dude. Lisa had been doing some calculating and realized that the competition wasn't over yet. Their scores were very close, and this last rider was going to mean the difference between winning and losing to The Dapper Dude. The Saddle Club sat next to one another on their horses and watched. Lisa didn't exactly want anything bad to happen to the final rider, but she did hope she'd mess up a bit. Lisa crossed her fingers. Then she looked at her friends' hands. They'd all crossed their fingers, too!

The final rider began and she was good. She wasn't as good as Kate, but she was good enough to make her team win. She rounded the barrels rapidly and her horse sprinted on the straightaways at a winning pace.

Lisa crossed the fingers of her other hand. She tried to cross her toes, but her boots were too tight. She concentrated on the rider. The girl rode very close to the barrels as she rounded them. It was the winning way. Each time, the barrel rocked a little bit, then settled back into its upright position. The girl headed for the final barrel. Her horse swept to the right and then turned left, closing in on the barrel as he went. As before, he brushed the barrel with his shoulder. As before, it rocked, ever so slightly. But then, unlike the first two barrels, the horse struck it with his hoof as he broke into a gallop for the final sprint.

The barrel tipped to the left. The crowd went "Ooooooh!" The barrel lurched to the right. The crowd went "Aaaaaah!" The barrel rolled forward. The crowd went "Uuuuuuuh!" The barrel rocked backward and tumbled onto its side.

The Bar None Riders went "Yippeeeeee!"

THE AWARDS CEREMONIES at The Two Mile Creek
Rodeo were very different from any awards ceremonies
Stevie, Carole, and Lisa had ever seen. In the horse
shows they were used to, the judges announced the
winners and when the winners stepped forward, somebody clipped a ribbon onto the horse's bridle. People
clapped politely and photographs were taken.

The rodeo was much showier. As winners were announced, the cowboys galloped out of the chute into
the center of the ring, waving hats and cheering
loudly. A couple of the winners even got their horses

to rear right in front of the judges. Carole loved every minute of it and it gave her an idea.

She told her teammates about it. They agreed it was the perfect finish.

But first, they had all kinds of chances to cheer for Eli. After all, he'd taken two first places and one second place. The crowd remembered him when he came out to accept his check for taking second place in the saddle-bronc riding, and they cheered for him and for The Bar None. Carole noticed Jeannie standing by the fence. Nobody was cheering louder or harder than she was. Eli waved to Jeannie from the center of the ring. The crowd loved that, too.

A few minutes later, Eli came out to accept his first-place prize for calf roping. He was grinning and waving even more proudly than before. But the biggest thrill for The Bar None Riders was when he came to accept his first-place prize for steer wrestling, because he didn't come out alone. Jeannie was with him! They were riding together on his horse. The crowd roared its approval. Eli seemed to like it, too, since Jeannie was holding on by squeezing him tightly around his waist!

It was nice, really nice, to see Eli and Jeannie so obviously happy. Carole was glad Stevie had done whatever it was she'd done that had made it work out.

There were other things Carole was glad about, too. She was glad that Lisa had ridden so well in the barrel race, because that had saved the team and won the event for them as much as Kate's outstanding ride. It made her feel proud to be part of a team that knew that teamwork meant doing your best no matter what happened.

"And now for the award to the winning barrel-race team, The Bar None Riders!"

Kate led them into the ring at a gallop. She circled around the arena and came to a stop in front of the judges. The other four girls kept riding at a lope next to her so that when people in the stands looked down, they saw riders and horses making The Bar None symbol:

$$\overline{}$$
O

The crowd was pleased with Carole's idea, and Carole smiled to herself in satisfaction. Not only was it appropriately showy for a rodeo, but it was also another way to remind everyone about The Bar None.

"We've got two prizes for these girls," the judge announced. "First, there's the award for winning the competition. Their overall team score was the best by just one-half of one second. It's not much, but it's enough, and these girls deserve a big hand."

Kate took the envelope and shook the judge's hand.

"The other award that goes to this team, or rather one member of this team, is the fastest individual score. Our judges couldn't believe their eyes when they saw this one, folks, so let's have a big, big hand for a newcomer to rodeo riding, but a true champion in many circles, Miss Kate Devine!"

The girls thought that was something to cheer about, too.

DINNER THAT NIGHT was the biggest celebration The Bar None had seen since the Devines had bought the place.

"I just had the feeling I should have some bubbly on ice," Phyllis said, bringing champagne out of the kitchen to accompany the gigantic sheet cake she'd made that said,

CONGRATULATIONS TO THE BEST, BAR NONE

—

O

There were six paying guests at the ranch for the rodeo weekend and they all seemed to be just as thrilled with the rodeo and the ranch's victory as the riders themselves. Christine's parents had been invited to join the celebration as well.

Frank poured champagne for the grown-ups and ginger ale for The Bar None Riders. Phyllis had just started cutting the cake when the phone rang.

Since Kate was the closest to it, she answered it. It was for Eli. She called him to the phone and returned to the dining room.

A few minutes later, Eli rejoined the group. There was an odd, flustered look on his face.

"Who was it?" Stevie asked.

Eli blushed. "It was the college," he said.

"Had they heard about the rodeo already?" Frank asked.

"I didn't know it, but their rodeo scout was there today. He came to watch me perform, but he had to leave right after it was over, so he didn't get a chance to talk to me."

"Boy, are you lucky!" Stevie said. "If you'd known he was there, you probably would have been so nervous you would have blown everything. I know I would have!"

"Well, I might have anyway," Eli said slowly.

"What do you mean?" Frank asked in a concerned voice. "Didn't you get accepted?"

"Yes, I got accepted."

"No scholarship, then? Is that the problem?"

"Oh, no, sir. I got a full rodeo scholarship, including expenses, for four years."

"Then I don't see the problem here, Eli. What's wrong?"

"Well, sir," Eli began, stammering as he tried to collect his thoughts to explain himself clearly. "You know how it is between a cowboy and his horse, don't you?"

"Oh, sure," Frank said. "If you want to use one of our horses at school, Eli, why, that'll be okay with Phyllis and me."

"I may do that, sir, but that's not what the problem is. See, today I found out that the same kind of thing can be true between a steer wrestler and his hazer—I mean in some special cases—like mine. I just don't see that I'd be doing myself any favors going to study rodeo work unless I could be with my rodeo partner—"

Everbody turned to look at Jeannie. She wasn't blushing at all. She was grinning happily.

"Eli Grimes, you go call that man right back and tell him you'll take the scholarship, every penny of it!"

"But Jeannie, without you—"

"What's this 'without me' stuff? I'll be there, too. I wouldn't go to college anyplace but where you're going. Besides,"—and now she did blush—"I applied there months ago. Now I can send in my acceptance, too."

Stevie was the first to laugh. It was so funny that she'd thought she was helping to get Eli and Jeannie together. She'd undoubtedly pushed their romance, but she'd underestimated Jeannie by quite a bit! That young woman was way ahead of Stevie when it came to scheming!

Pretty soon everybody was laughing. It seemed that now there was even more to cheer about and celebrate.

"Well," Eli said. "As long as I've got this full scholarship, Frank, I want you and Phyllis to have my rodeo winnings to help you out here, same as you've helped me out."

He handed Frank the envelope. Frank shook Eli's hand and then gave him a hug. "Thanks," was all he could say.

Stevie nudged Kate. It was their turn. "Here, Dad," Kate said, giving him the two envelopes the judges had given her.

"Why, Kate!" her mother said. "We can't take the money from you girls."

Carole spoke for them all. "Please take it, Phyllis," she said. "We just entered the contest for The Bar None. Whether we won or lost wasn't as important to us as doing something for the ranch. It's our way of saying thank you, so the only thing you can do is to say 'you're welcome.' "

"And you *are* welcome. All of you, anytime," Phyllis said.

"Say, girls, is there anything in particular you'd like to see us use this money for?" Frank asked.

"How about a game of Pictionary?" Stevie suggested. The other girls began giggling. "I mean, it'll help you keep that competitive edge. . . ."

Frank looked at her curiously. Stevie hoped he wasn't going to ask her to explain, because there was no way she could. But she didn't have to. Frank smiled. "Sure thing, Stevie. Pictionary it is." Then he turned to his other guests. "Now, I think it's time to get on with our celebration. Who needs cake?"

"OH, I HATE reality!" Stevie complained three days later. She and Lisa and Carole were having a Saddle Club meeting at the local ice cream parlor, Tastee Delight, better known as TD's, following their regular Tuesday lesson at Pine Hollow.

They were all back home in Willow Creek. The weather was still cold, and the schools were open again. In other words, home didn't have too much going for it.

"Don't you wish we were still relaxing on The Bar None?" Lisa smiled.

"Yes, I do," Stevie said. "Being there is nicer than being here."

"Especially when there's no school?" Carole asked.

"That's right. Definitely when there's no school."

The waitress arrived to take their orders. "Oh, it's you," she said when she spotted Stevie.

Stevie smiled sweetly at her.

"What's it going to be this time?" the waitress asked. "Caramel on Bubble Gum? Bubble Gum on Blueberry Treat? Marshmallow on Watermelon Ice?"

Stevie was famous for ordering odd combinations of flavors. Her friends sometimes suspected she did it so other people wouldn't take tastes of her ice cream. The waitress at TD's seemed to think Stevie did it just to upset her stomach!

What Carole and Lisa liked best about Stevie's orders was that she invariably did it with a straight face.

"Oh!" Stevie said to the waitress. "Have you tried the Marshmallow on Watermelon? Do you recommend it?"

The woman paled. Stevie smiled sweetly. "I have to think a minute," Stevie said.

Lisa ordered a vanilla frozen yogurt with sliced bananas on top. Carole asked for a dish of chocolate ice cream with some almonds sprinkled on it. The waitress looked back at Stevie.

"I'll just have a dish of vanilla," Stevie decided.

"No sauce?" the waitress asked.

"No, just plain."

The waitress smiled.

"Well, on second thought, I'll have some chocolate sprinkles, too," Stevie said. The waitress jotted that down. "And some almonds, too. Oh, and maybe a few banana slices, why not. And a touch of that blueberry syrup. And just a spoonful of marshmallow fluff. And a teeny smidgen of caramel. Do you still have the boysenberry sauce? Some of that, too. And then of course, a cherry, and—"

The waitress fled.

"Well, what's the matter with her?" Stevie said.

"She probably needs a week's vacation at The Bar None," Lisa suggested.

"Probably," Stevie said, recalling what they were talking about earlier. "It is restful there, isn't it?"

Carole leaned forward and put her elbows on the table. "Well, that depends on what you call restful," she said. "It seems to me we didn't do an awful lot of resting while we were there."

"We didn't spend one minute of time in school," Stevie pointed out.

"Yes, but we did an awful lot of other things," Lisa said. "I mean, we began as a major spy ring at The Dapper Dude. We learned a whole new riding skill, barrel racing, we camped out on a mountain in the desert, we unearthed a wicked plot by the wranglers at the rival ranch, we rode in a parade, we won a whole rodeo event—"

"We helped save The Bar None, we welcomed a new member to The Saddle Club, western branch," Carole continued.

"And we put a pair of lovebirds together," Stevie said proudly.

"All in all, a pretty restful week," Lisa joked.

"There's one thing I'm wondering about," Carole said.

"What's that?" Stevie asked.

"If we're so clever and can do all these things, how come we can't make the pipes at our school burst more often so we can go back to the ranch soon?"

"Give me time," Stevie said thoughtfully. "I'll think of something!"

Carole and Lisa looked at each other and grinned. They had no doubt she would.

ABOUT THE AUTHOR

BONNIE BRYANT is the author of more than thirty books for young readers, including the best-selling novelizations of *The Karate Kid* movies and *Teenage Mutant Ninja Turtles*. The Saddle Club books are her first for Bantam Skylark. She wrote her first book eight years ago and has been busy at her word processor ever since. (For her first three years as an author, Ms. Bryant was also working in the office of a publishing company. In 1986, she left her job to write full-time.)

Whenever she can, Ms. Bryant goes horseback riding in her hometown, New York City. She's had many riding experiences in the city's Central Park that have found their way into her Saddle Club books—and lots which haven't!

The author has two sons, and they all live together in an apartment in Greenwich Village that is just too small for a horse.

Holidays are for good times and parties.
But the best times are spent with best friends.
The best times are

Make plans to spend the holidays with
The Saddle Club,™ *The Fabulous Five*, and the **Petite Naté**™
Bath Collection. Petite Naté has fun products to make you
look your absolute best. A wonderfully scented cologne
that you can splash or spray on, bubbles and shampoo
to turn your bath into an adventure,
talc and lotion for after-bath fun.

Share this great gift idea with your best friend. Look for
'Twice the Fun,' a holiday gift collection—from Petite Naté:
includes the Petite Naté JUST FOR GIRLS Book featuring
two stories from *The Saddle Club*™ and *The Fabulous Five*
PLUS Petite Naté Spray-On Soft Cologne.
Find it this holiday season wherever Petite Naté is sold.

And look for the Petite Naté JUST FOR GIRLS Book
in specially-marked Holiday Gift Sets wherever
Bantam Books are sold.

Petite Naté is available in the U.S. and Puerto Rico.

Saddle up for great reading with

THE SADDLE CLUB

A blue-ribbon series by Bonnie Bryant

Stevie, Carole and Lisa are all very different, but they *love* horses! The three girls are best friends at Pine Hollow Stables, where they ride and care for all kinds of horses. Come to Pine Hollow and get ready for all the fun and adventure that comes with being 13!

- ☐ 15594 **HORSE CRAZY #1** $2.75
- ☐ 15611 **HORSE SHY #2** $2.75
- ☐ 15626 **HORSE SENSE #3** $2.75
- ☐ 15637 **HORSE POWER #4** $2.75
- ☐ 15703 **TRAIL MATES #5** $2.75
- ☐ 15728 **DUDE RANCH #6** $2.75
- ☐ 15754 **HORSE PLAY #7**..$2.75
- ☐ 15769 **HORSE SHOW #8** $2.75
- ☐ 15780 **HOOF BEAT #9**..$2.75
- ☐ 15790 **RIDING CAMP #10**......................................$2.75
- ☐ 15805 **HORSE WISE #11** $2.75
- ☐ 15821 **RODEO RIDER BOOK #12**......................$2.75

Watch for other SADDLE CLUB books all year. More great reading—and riding to come!

Buy them at your local bookstore or use this handy page for ordering.

Taffy Sinclair is perfectly gorgeous and totally stuck-up. Ask her rival Jana Morgan or anyone else in the sixth grade of Mark Twain Elementary. Once you meet Taffy, life will **never** be the same.

Don't Miss Any of the Terrific Taffy Sinclair Titles from Betsy Haynes!

- ☐ 15819 **TAFFY GOES TO HOLLYWOOD** $2.95
- ☐ 15712 **THE AGAINST TAFFY SINCLAIR CLUB** $2.75
- ☐ 15693 **BLACKMAILED BY TAFFY SINCLAIR** $2.75
- ☐ 15604 **TAFFY SINCLAIR AND THE MELANIE MAKEOVER** $2.75
- ☐ 15644 **TAFFY SINCLAIR AND THE ROMANCE MACHINE DISASTER** $2.75
- ☐ 15714 **TAFFY SINCLAIR AND THE SECRET ADMIRER EPIDEMIC** $2.75
- ☐ 15713 **TAFFY SINCLAIR, BABY ASHLEY AND ME** $2.75
- ☐ 15647 **TAFFY SINCLAIR, QUEEN OF THE SOAPS** $2.75
- ☐ 15645 **TAFFY SINCLAIR STRIKES AGAIN** $2.75
- ☐ 15607 **THE TRUTH ABOUT TAFFY SINCLAIR** $2.75

Follow the adventures of Jana and the rest of **THE FABULOUS FIVE** in a new series by Betsy Haynes.

Great FREE offer
just for you!

Join SNEAK PEEKS™!

Do you want to know what's new before anyone else? Do you like to read great books about girls just like you? If you do, then you won't want to miss SNEAK PEEKS™! Be the first of your friends to know what's hot ... When you join SNEAK PEEKS™, we'll send you FREE inside information in the mail about the latest books ... *before they're published!* Plus updates on your favorite series, authors, and exciting new stories filled with friendship and fun ... adventure and mystery ... girlfriends and boyfriends.

It's easy to be a member of SNEAK PEEKS™. Just fill out the coupon below ... and get ready for fun! It's FREE! Don't delay—sign up today!